rat medicine
& other unlikely curatives

rat medicine
& other unlikely curatives

Lauren B. Davis

Lauren B. Davis

To Edwin + Noreen,
Wonderful evening with new friends!
Lauren
Paris 2003

Mosaic Press
OAKVILLE, ON • NIAGARA FALLS, NY

Canadian Cataloguing in Publication Data

Davis, Lauren B., 1955-
    Rat medicine and other unlikely curatives

ISBN 0-88962-690-1

I. Title.

PS8557.A8384R37 1999   C813'.54   C99-932645-7
R9199.3.D3125R37 1999

Rat Medicine has been previously published in *Exile, Smoke and Ash* has been previously published in *Room of One's Own, Drop in Any Time* has been previously published in *The Queen Street Quarterly*.

Published by MOSAIC PRESS, offices and warehouse at 1252 Speers Road, Units #1 & 2, Oakville, Ontario, L6L 5N9,Canada, and Mosaic Press, 4500 Witmer Industrial Estates, PMB 145, Niagara Falls, NY 14305-1386, U.S.A.

Mosaic Press acknowledges the assistance of the Canada Council, the Ontario Arts Council and the Department of Canadian Heritage,Government of Canada for their support of our publishing programme.

Le Conseil des Arts   The Canada Council
        du Canada   for the Arts

MOSAIC PRESS, in Canada:
1252 Speers Road,
Units #1 & 2,
Oakville, Ontario, L6L 5N9
Phone / Fax: 905-825-2130
cp507@freenet.toronto.on.ca

MOSAIC PRESS, in USA:
4500 Witmer Industrial Estates
PMB 145, Niagara Falls, NY
14305-1386
Phone/Fax:1-800-387-8992
cp507@freenet.toronto.on.ca

table of contents

acknowledgements

I would like to thank David Applefield for his kindness, support and keen editorial eye. This manuscript would never have seen the light of day without him. I'd also like to thank Howard Aster and everyone at Mosaic Press for their continuing encouragement of new writers.

My heartfelt thanks also to Timothy Findley, whose warm mentoring and wisdom have been gifts beyond measure; and to Marnie Woodrow for morale boosting e-mails, and friendship.

I thank Susan Tiberghien and all the folks at the Geneva Writer's Group.

And Kenneth Grey, who is my reference for all things hip, and makes the act of writing a much less lonely experience. A rare good friend.

And of course, to Susan Applewhaite, my love and gratitude for always believing in me. A faithful friend and cheerleader for far more years than either of us is willing to admit.

This book is dedicated to my husband, Ron

Rat Medicine

I saw the first rat next to where we stored the chicken feed. It was a week before John used his fists on me. I was out by the sacks and felt like somebody was watching me. The hair stood up on places of my body where I didn't know I had hair. I put down the tin pail I used to scatter the feed and picked up a shovel leaning against the shed. We'd never had no trouble. Living so far out of town like we did criminal types didn't seem to have the gumption to haul ass all the way out to our place, but there was always a first time. I turned around and there he was, sitting back on his hindquarters like a little rat-dog begging for a titbit, up on the shed roof. He didn't flick a whisker, bold as brass. Just kept looking at me, his little front paws tucked up in front of his belly, his eyes bright as black glass.

"What do you think you're doing up there?" I said, but of course the rat didn't say nothing back.

"Don't think you can get in and eat up all this good feed." The rat kept looking at me, straight and firm like.

"We got a big old tom cat round here. He's going be picking his teeth with your bones, my friend."

Lauren B. Davis

If rats could be said to smirk, that's what he was doing.

Now, most people, they really hate rats. Not me. I don't hate nothing about the animal kingdom. Not snakes, not spiders, not coyote, not buzzard. That's the Ojibway blood, from my mother's people. My Granny used to tell me, you dream about a rat, you dreaming about some sickness, maybe a bad one, soon to come on. Granny was usually right about these things. I set store in omens, in symbols and signs. It's all there if you know what to look for. So I looked at the rat, recognised it for a fellow who'd come to tell me something.

"You got news for me, rat man? If you do, you better tell me. I ain't got all day." The rat cleaned behind his ears. Then he turned and stuck his bald tail straight in the air and disappeared toward the other side of the shed roof. I tried to get around to see where he was going, fast as my size would allow, but when I looked there weren't no sign of him.

I didn't tell John about the rat because I knew he'd just blame it on me. Tell me I didn't keep the place clean enough. Which was a lie, but true facts never mattered much to John when he got a good rage going. I got a couple of old oil drums John kept about the place and put the sacks of feed in there, put old boards on the top and weighted them down with rocks.

When John came back that night he was in a mood even fouler than the night before. His moods had been getting worse for some time. He slammed the screen door so hard I thought the wood frame'd splinter.

"Nell!" he yelled. "This place looks like a goddamn pigsty! What the hell do you do all day?"

There wasn't no point in answering. He was just looking for a fight.

"C'mon in here and get your dinner, John."

He sat down at the kitchen table, his filthy work boots leaving marks on my clean floor. He stank of sweat from working at the mill in this heat. 'Course he wouldn't have thought to wash up before dinner. I didn't dare say nothing. I served us both up our food and set the plates down on the table.

"Fat as you are," John said, "don't think you're going to be

2

eating all that. Take half off, Nell. You need to loose some goddamn weight."

I just looked at him.

"I mean it. You are getting to be a big fat squaw. I can't hardly bear to look at you."

I am a big woman, I don't deny it. I wasn't always this size, though I never have been small. It was after John Jr. died that I really started packing it on. Seemed like I didn't want to do much more than try and fill up the hole his dying left. Slipped away in his sleep, silent as a leaf falling in the dark and him not a year old. But I found a way to keep going without turning mean, turning against the force of life. Which is more than I can say for his father. We'd lost the baby more'n three years then and John never did get over it.

That and the farm failing.

John said the reason the farm failed, why the crops all withered up and got ate by every sort of crawling creature, was the land was poison. Said the poison came from up the mine that started digging great wounds in the side of South Mountain. Well I don't know. Maybe yes, and maybe no. It wasn't that John didn't work hard, it's just he never had his father's touch. Everything just turned to rot as soon as he came near it. It made him bitter.

The worst was last month, when we couldn't make the mortgage. It hurt his pride, faced with the choice to go down to Rickett's mill and beg for work, or hand over the land that'd been in his family for generations to the bank. It was hard on a man, sure hard. Years of too little money and too much whiskey and a small town where a man could never get ahead of his reputation. John liked his whiskey more and more. Me, I never touched the stuff. My mother and grandmother both impressed on me that you didn't get to be no spirit walker with a bottle in your hand. That might be OK for whites, but it wasn't for Indians.

So I tried to understand. That's the way women are, I think, that's the medicine we carry. To try to understand a man and stay soft about it. But that don't mean the hurts aren't there, deep in the marrow.

Lauren B. Davis

I looked across the table and saw the contempt in his face. I scraped half my food off my plate, but it didn't matter. I'd lost my appetite anyway.

That night I dreamed about a rat. It was sitting on the roof, like some sort of weather vane. It faced east and its nose scented every little breeze that came along.

Three days later I was washing dishes, up to my arms in warm, soap-creamy water. I like washing dishes; it's like meditation, just looking out the window at the back garden. That year I'd put in nasturtiums, because I like their peppery taste and they look so pretty. I got a crop of the Three Sisters: corn, beans and squash, plus tomatoes, zucchini, carrots and such, set about with a border of marigolds to keep down the bugs. I have a good hand at gardens, although I don't brag about it, because it sets John off to distraction the way things just seem to jump to life under my fingers.

So, anyway, there I am, looking out the window and daydreaming about the sorts of things a women daydreams about when her man don't want to touch her anymore, and I realise there's a face in the window looking back at me. A rat face. There's the bugger, just sitting on the windowsill, staring me down. His fur's all clean and glossy brown and he's got a white stomach and little pink ears. He reaches out and puts one little paw up against the glass. I put my finger up against the glass on my side. He doesn't budge and the two of us stay like that for a minute or so, like somebody visiting a prisoner in a jail, although it was hard to figure out who was who. I had half a mind to open the window up and let him in; I was almost getting fond of the little guy.

Lying out on warm stones back of the house was Oscar, our tomcat, and the mouser supreme. He stretched himself into one of those contortions only cats can do, all sinew and pretzel.

"You better get gone, little buddy," I said to the rat. The rat just looked at me and put both paws up on the window. I tapped on the glass, trying to scare him off. Oscar often jumped up on the sill so I could open the window and let him in, and I didn't

4

want to see the little guy get eaten up. "Go on! Go on!" I hissed, trying not to draw Oscar's attention. Too late. Oscar was hightailing it over, ready to pounce on the rat. I closed my eyes.

Next thing I heard was Oscar's whining meow, demanding to be let in. I opened my eyes, figuring the rat had taken a quick dive out of there. On one end of the ledge was Oscar, as expected, but on the other end, not a foot away, was the rat. Calm as a cream-fed cat himself, eyes directly on me. Oscar didn't even notice. I opened the window to let Oscar in, wondering if the rat planned on jumping in as well, but he stayed put. Oscar scattered in, upsetting a glass left to dry on the drain board. I dove to grab it before it fell to the floor. When I turned back, the rat was gone. I shook my head and looked at Oscar.

"Well, some fine hunter you are, you big hairball." Oscar looked at me with the same complete lack of interest he always has, unless there's fish guts involved.

That night, John threw his plate of food over my head where it shattered into a hundred pieces. Said the chops were burned, which was nonsense. He shoved me up against the counter and smeared a dishrag in my face. Told me to clean it up and fix him something decent to eat. By the time I cleaned it up and cooked him some new chops, crying all the while, he'd passed out in the Barcalounger in front of the TV with a bottle of Jack Daniels in his fist. I put a blanket over him and left him there.

That night I dreamed a swarm of rats were churning under our bed, their tails all tied together in knots.

In the morning I had a big purple bruise on my hip from where I connected with the counter. I had five small, separate storm cloud-coloured bruises on my upper arm. As I fixed John coffee and eggs and didn't talk to him at all, he came up behind me and, seeing the marks, kissed every one of them and said he was sorry. His damp lips felt so good on my parched skin.

"I'm sorry baby, I'm sorry," he kept muttering. I could have sworn he shed a tear.

John is a good-looking man. The first time I saw him, coming to buy smoked fish off my Uncle Joe, and me only eighteen at the time, I was a goner. This big old cowboy in the skin-tight jeans was the one for me. Looked just like Clint Eastwood. Auntie Betty said I was crazy to go off and marry some white man. We didn't know his family stories, didn't know what kind of past he was hauling around with him. But I didn't care. My eyes were firmly focused on his round little white man's butt in those Levi's.

"I don't know why you put up with me sometimes," he said and cradled my face in his big callused hands. He said he was sorry again and took me in his arms right there in the kitchen. I forgave him. You bet I did.

Two days later I was sitting in the kitchen having coffee with my friend Joelle when I look up over her shoulder to the top of the refrigerator and what do I see but my rat pal looking out at me from in between the fat chef cookie jar and the empty plastic ice cube trays.

"I'll be damned. Joelle, turn around slow and look up on the top of the 'fridge."

"What?" she said.

"Up there, look! Look at that damn rat!"

"Rat!" she shrieked. "What rat?"

"There, right there - look at it!"

"What are you talking about? I don't see no rat."

"You don't see him. Right there. That rat?" The rat sat up on his haunches, spit into his paws and gave himself a good old cleaning.

"Where are you looking?"

"There, goddamn it! Washing his ears!" I pointed frantically.

"I don't know what you're smoking, but there is no rat on the refrigerator. You're giving me the creeps."

Now there were two of them. Something caught my eye. I looked over by the sink and there was another one.

"You don't see anything at all strange in this kitchen?" I asked.

"The only strange thing in this kitchen is *you*."

When Joelle left, I called over to the rez. I called my Auntie Betty.

"I got rat problems." I said.

"You got rats," Auntie Betty said, practical as always, "you got to go out to the field they live in and explain to them you ain't got no extras to go round but you'll try and leave them out some of what you can spare if they agree to respect your stores."

"Ain't that kind of rat," I said.

"Well, what kind are they?"

"The kind only I can see. And I been dreaming about them, too."

"Oh. That kind of rat." She paused. "I'll call you back."

I knew she was going to go pray some and ask her spirits what was going on over at my place. I'm not as good at this direct stuff as she is. I drank two more cups of tea waiting for the phone to ring.

"You got problems in your house, eh?" she said. "You got marriage problems."

"Yeah, I know."

"He's got some bad stuff around him. Very dark stuff."

I didn't say anything. I remembered the look on his face when he threw the plate.

"He's got anger twisted up in him, that one. You got to be careful. You know what I mean?"

"What should I do?"

"What you asking me that for? You gonna listen to me? You gonna come back home? You gonna leave that white man?"

I didn't answer.

"Uh-huh," Auntie Betty said. "I thought so. OK, now you listen to me. Animals don't take the time out of their busy day unless they got serious business. You hear me?"

"I hear."

"You got to listen to them. You got a bad sickness coming into your house. You need to clear things out. I don't know if it's too far gone, but you got to smudge out your house good. You got sweetgrass? You got sage?"

"Yeah."

"Well, use 'em. Smoke that house up good, smoke your bed up good. Put a red blanket on the bed."

"OK."

"Then you go get these plants and boil 'em up. Drink the tea." She named some herbs and plants.

"One thing, Nell. One thing I got to ask. Is he hitting you?"

"Naw. Not really."

"What the hell is 'not really'! Either he is, or he ain't! You better get ready. His anger's gonna bust out all over you. I'll do what I can, but I don't know. You should come home for a while."

"I can't. I love him, Auntie."

"Love! Phooey! Should go back to the old ways! Let your aunties pick you out a good red man. Stay where we can keep an eye on you! You young people! All the same!" She went on for a while, but I didn't listen much. I knew this part by heart. And besides, I was too busy watching the rats run back and forth from the bedroom to the bathroom.

"Nell? You listening?"

"Yes, Auntie."

"OK, one last thing. Fat as you are these days, you ain't gonna be able to dodge him if he comes at you. You offer to-bacco to these rats and ask them for a tuft of their hair. You braid it into your hair. That'll make you nimble like they are. Give you a chance if you need it."

"I never heard that one before."

"Yeah, well, it ain't strictly ours, eh? That one's from Africa. I learned it from that black nurse works with me midwifing. We trade stuff sometimes. Don't matter. All the same medicine. You just use it, you hear? Spirit rats or flesh and blood, they'll give you what you need. They're here to help."

"Yes, Auntie."

I promised to call her tomorrow and made her promise not to tell my mother, not to tell my brothers, for what good it would do? I knew how gossip passed around out on the rez. Wouldn't be long before everybody knew what was going on at my house. Which maybe wasn't such a bad thing. Get a few of the old timers burning tobacco for me. Long as my brother Jimmy didn't find out. He'd be over wanting to kick some white man's butt.

I went out and offered my tobacco and found a tuft of rat fur up on the windowsill. I braided it in my hair. I picked the herbs.

I drank the tea. I smudged the house. I put the red blanket on the bed.

It was Sunday the next day, and I knew John'd be out drinking with his buddies late that night. It could go either way. Maybe he'd just come home and pass out. Maybe he'd come home mean. I slept with one eye open, tucked up under the protection blanket. I didn't see no rats, but didn't know if that was a good thing or a bad. Rats abandon a sinking ship, or a house where there's a fire coming.

I heard the truck skid through the gravel around 3:00 a.m. He was drunk as a cowboy after a long dry cattle drive. He came in the kitchen, slamming stuff around and stumbling and cursing as he barked his shins and banged his elbows. I heard him pissing in the bathroom, then heard him coming down the hall. He stood in the doorway a few minutes, swaying. I knew he couldn't see my open eyes, dark as the room was, and I sure wasn't going to close them, not knowing what was coming. He took a couple of wide-legged steps toward the bed, trying to keep his balance, and finally toppled like a cut pine across my body. I heaved him over and left him snoring on top of the red blanket. Man, he smelled bad. Whiskey and smoke and beer and, although it broke my heart to admit it, some woman other than me.

I got up and went to the living room and cried myself to sleep, dreaming about rats on river rafts and rats in sewer drains and rats caught in traps.

I woke up the next morning to the sound of John puking. I went to fix him some coffee and orange juice, figuring that'd be about all his stomach could handle. I reached into the cupboard to get his favourite mug, the big one with the bucking bronco on the side of it. Sitting in it, with his little pink paws hooked over the top, was the rat.

"Morning, little buddy." I said. The rat jumped out and stood next to the coffee-pot. I opened the 'fridge to get the orange juice. A rat sat on the stack of cheese slices. He didn't budge when I reached in. I wondered if he'd learned how to turn the light on in there when the door was closed.

I heard John behind me and turned. He was still in his boots, his jeans, only his shirt was gone, and I guess he'd puked on it. Even mad at him as I was there was a twinge down in my belly at the sight of his naked chest, all hard muscle and sinew, his stomach flat, with pale golden hair running down into the top of his jeans. There was a rat sitting on the top of his head, yanking up his hair between its long pointy teeth.

"Oh man. My head's killing me." His eyes were bloodshot and yellowish, like two ketchup-covered eggs with runny yolks.

"Serves you right." I wanted him to be hurting. I handed him his coffee. The rat on his head jumped off and disappeared into the living room.

"I ain't in the mood, Nell."

"But I guess you were in the mood last night." I stood with my hands on my hips. I could feel the hurt starting to switch around to righteous anger. I knew I should keep my mouth shut, but I was too mad, too hurt.

"Leave it alone." His voice was ragged and dangerous.

"I don't want to leave it alone. You smelled like a goddamn whorehouse when you came in last night, you bastard. I want to know who you been with!" Out of the corner of my eye I could see flurries of rat fur, diving under counters, through the window, skittering around door jams and out of the room.

He slammed the cup down on the table, sloshing the coffee over the rim. His hands balled up into fists. He leaned towards me.

"Well you can bet your fat ass it was somebody under 200 pounds."

Tears sprang to my eyes and my face went red.

"Look at yourself, you think any man'd want you?" He ran his eyes up and down my body and sneered. "You used to be a good looking woman, but now you ain't nothing but a sack of lard."

"I am a good wife to you, John McBride. I can't help it if I gained weight."

"What the hell do you mean, you can't help it? I ain't the one stuffing food down your throat! If you'd get off your floppy ass and do some work around this place, maybe you'd lose some of it, maybe I'd want you again!"

"I do all the work around this place! You don't spend long enough here to do no work."

"You saying I'm to blame for how disgusting you got? You blaming me, bitch?"

He took two steps toward me and I backed up until I found myself against the counter.

"I ain't blaming you, but goddamn John, it ain't me who's the problem here - it's you!" I couldn't stop myself. "Out whoring around, mean drunk all the time - I ain't gonna take it no more, you understand?"

I didn't even see the blow coming.

Even with the rat-fur charm braided in my hair, I couldn't duck the first punch or the second, or the one after that. I lost count then. He went for my face, I guess, because it would be the place where the hurt would show the most. Proof that there was some small spot in the world where he could have an effect. My nose. My lips. My cheeks.

I went down and, a gal my size... well, I went down hard and stayed down. I could see his boots in flashes of motion, misted in red.

I think it was all this flesh that saved me from getting worse than I got, and that was bad enough. But I was bundled way down deep inside the womb of myself and even though his hands left bruises, they didn't break no bones. It didn't hurt. I kept thinking it should hurt more, but it just felt like numbness everywhere, great stains of frozen places bursting out from under his icy fists and feet.

"John, John,..." I just kept repeating in a whisper. My heart speaking to his, willing him to hear me, to see me, to stop. *You're breaking me, I thought, you're breaking me apart.* Then everything went quiet.

I could hear ragged breathing, great gulps of wet sobbing air. I thought it was me, but my moans were underneath that lung-punctured sound. I took my hands away from my face and as I did I heard my Auntie's voice, steel-strong and even.

"You step back, John McBride. Step back now."

11

I looked up at my husband. He stood over me, his face a twisted, crooked thing. Tears poured down his cheeks. His stomach heaved. He looked down at me as though he had no idea of how I'd fallen. He brought his bloody fists up in front of his own eyes and began to howl like a wild dog. He pounded his own face, first with his right hand, then his left, sparing no force.

"Bastard!" he cried. "Bastard!"

"Stop this! Stop this now! You hear me!" Auntie Betty stood in the doorway behind John. She filled the space with her square bulk. Her long grey braid was decorated with megis shells. She was dressed for serious ceremony work. Ribbons in her spirit colours on her skirt and blouse. Medicine pouch. In her left hand she carried the hawk wing fan, in her right the sweetgrass basket containing her pipe, tobacco, other things known only to her.

John hit himself square in the face with both fists.

Auntie Betty put her basket down and walked up behind him. She reached up and smacked him on the back of the head.

"Don't be any more of a jackass than you already are. There's been enough hitting for one day, eh?" She glared at him as he spun around. She raised the hawk wing fan and fluttered a circle in the air around his head. John let out a strangled noise, clamped his hand to his mouth and pushed past her out the door. I heard retching noises.

"Good. Puke up all that bad stuff," said Auntie Betty, coming toward me. "Come on little one, let's see what kind of shape you're in." She bent down and helped haul me to my feet. I was shaky. There was blood on my dress, dripping down from my nose.

"Looks like I got here just in time. You'll live. Could hear it in the wind this morning. Time to come visit. Had Jimmy drop me off in the truck down the road a ways. Didn't think this'd be the time for him to come calling." She leaned me up against the counter and ran the tap water good and cold. She wet down a tea towel and put it in my hand. "Press that up against your face. You need ice." She waddled her wide, bow-legged walk to the 'fridge.

I started to cry, salty tears burning my split lip. The pickup tires squealed as John skidded out the drive and down the road.

"Don't waste your time crying, girl." She rolled ice in a plastic baggie. "Here, use this. What we need is a cup of tea. He's not coming back for a while. I guarantee. Sit," she ordered.

I did as I was told as she puttered around my kitchen and fixed the tea. She reached into her basket and took out a hide pouch, sprinkled some herbs into the teapot.

"This'll help the hurts, inside and out."

I didn't feel much of anything just then, except glad Auntie Betty was there, glad someone else was taking control of things. I felt as limp as a newborn baby and just as naked. We drank the tea. I held the ice to my swelling-up eye. Auntie Betty held my hand.

Later, she reached into her basket.

"I brought this for you," she said, and laid a carton of rat poison on the counter. "You got yourself a vermin problem."

"Poison?" I knew Auntie would never suggest such a thing, it went against the natural respect she had for one of all-her-relations, spirit rats or full bone and fur.

"I don't need that," I said, my chest tight as a drum.

"I think you do. You got these kinda rats, you got to get rid of 'em. White man's rats need white man's measures. This here's white man's poison."

"You can't be serious. You've lost your mind!"

"No, and you better remember to respect your elders! I ain't lost my mind, but you better start using yours. I ain't talking about poisoning nobody, not that some people don't deserve it," she snorted with disdain, "but I been giving it some thought. Rat spirit chose to show up here, not no other. No bear or wolf or snake. "

"You're scaring me, Auntie, and I been scared enough for one day."

"Well, let it be the last day anything scares you. You shed that fear skin and maybe you'll shed that fat skin too. Oh, don't look at me that way, you know it's true. Big woman's a fine thing, but not the way you're going at it. You can't grow another baby in you by trying to stuff if down your mouth. You weren't meant to be as big as you are, you ain't got the bones for it, not like me." She patted her belly and cackled. "But that'll take care of itself once you start taking care of yourself, and for now, that means getting rid of this big old rat."

"He didn't mean it. You saw how sorry he was. It's the pressure. We been going through some hard times."

"What a load of horse shit! Times is always hard. That ain't no excuse for what that man's doing. He needs to learn."

"I can't leave him."

"You can and you will. He might be able to get away with taking out his shit on soft-minded little white women, but no Indian woman's gonna stand for it." She leaned over and took both my hands in hers, looked into my battered up face.

"You think he's gonna stop unless you make him stop? You think it's not going to just get worse? Don't you watch Oprah?"

I didn't say nothing.

"Nellie. Answer me. You think it's gonna get any better unless he knows he's gone too far, knows exactly what it's cost him? Look me in the eye and tell me that."

She was right. I knew she was right and it caved in my heart to know it.

"I know."

"Well then."

"But Auntie, I…"

"Don't you even think about telling me you love that man! The man you fell in love with is gone. I don't know whether he'll be back or not, but what you got living in this house with you at the moment sure as hell is not a man to love. This is an evil thing, all twisted over on itself." I made a motion to protest. "Don't interrupt me. Sometimes you put poison out for rats and like magic they disappear. Seems like they know it just ain't safe no more." She looked at me, her eyes flashing like stars among the wrinkles. "You understand?"

And I did.

She stayed all afternoon and as night fell she smudged the house up good. Then she called Jimmy and had him pick her up. She waited out at the end of the driveway so he wouldn't come in and see me. Jimmy'd be just as likely to go off into town with his rifle and look for John, and nobody wanted that kind of trouble.

John didn't come home that night, and I shouldn't have expected him because Auntie Betty'd told me as much. Still, I lay in bed all night straining to hear the sound of his tires on the gravel. I finally fell asleep around dawn, too tired to mind the aches and pains, and didn't dream about nothing at all.

The next day I fasted. I smudged the house again. Around my neck I put the leather pouch with the lightening stone in it that Auntie'd given me. She'd dug up the round red stone from between the roots of a tree where lightening'd struck last spring. It was powerful protection. I wore my ribbon dress. Green ribbons, white ribbons, black and rose. This was my ceremony.

I fixed the food just so. All the things John liked. Fried chicken. Lima beans. Mashed potatoes. Carrot salad with raisins.

I heard the truck in the yard just before 6:00. I took a deep breath. Smoothed my hair. Said a prayer. I heard the screen door shut and then John was in the kitchen. He stood in the doorway, a bunch of red roses in his hand. He was wearing the shirt I'd given his brother Philip last Christmas, so I knew where he'd spent the night. His hair was combed down neat. He looked like a school kid showing up at my door to pick me up for a date.

"Jesus Nellie, I'm so sorry. I'm gonna spend the rest of my life making it up to you, I swear." He winced when he looked at me. My left eye was swollen and black, my lips were swollen, my cheek had a big bruise on it. I looked a mess. He didn't mention my clothes, although I was in what he called "squaw gear."

"Come on, baby. You just got to forgive me. It'll never happen again, I mean it, cross my heart. Here, sweetheart." He held out the flowers. I took them but didn't say nothing. I put them in the sink. He came to put his arms around me from behind. I cringed as he squeezed my bruised ribs.

"Don't," I said.

"OK, OK. I'm sorry." He put his hands up like I was holding a gun on him and backed away. "Christ. I really am sorry, baby.

I don't know what got into me. You know how much I love you."

"I fixed some food for you. Fried chicken. Your favourites," I said.

"Oh, Honey, you're just the best. I knew you wouldn't stay mad at me." He hugged me and this time I let him. His arms felt so good. For a second I felt safe there. Then I pushed him away.

"Sit down."

John swung his long leg over the back of the chrome chair and sat, a grin on his face. I opened the oven and brought the plate I'd kept warming over to him. Then I went back and leaned up against the kitchen counter, next to the open box of rat poison. He picked up his knife and fork.

"Where's yours?" he said.

"I'm not eating. This here's special food. Just for you, eh?"

"I don't want to eat alone, sugar."

"But I want you to."

He looked puzzled. He looked down at his plate. Looked back over to me and then his eyes flicked to the box of poison. The colour drained out of his face.

"No," he said.

"Why not?" I asked, folding my arms against my chest.

"You eat it," he said.

"Fine," I said. "See, it just don't matter to me anymore." I made a move toward the table, leaned over the plate, brushing my heavy breasts against his shoulder. I took the fork out of his hand and shovelled up a gob of mashed potatoes. I chewed it up and swallowed. He looked at me. I offered him the fork.

"Go ahead," I said.

"No. Eat some of the chicken."

I cut off a piece of chicken and ate it. "Um, um. I sure am a good cook. Yessir. That's one thing you're gonna miss."

He pushed his chair away from the table and stood up.

"What're you talking about?"

"I'm going home John. I'm leaving you." I felt it then. Knew my heart had just broken.

"You ain't going nowhere." The colour rushed back into his face, his eyes dark and cloudy.

"Yes I am. And, John McBride, you're going to let me walk out that door and drive back to where you found me. You know why?" I walked back over to the counter and stood near the poison. "Because if you don't, you will never eat another meal in this house without wondering. You will never get another good night's sleep."

"Bitch!" he said, in a rush of air like he'd been punched. He made a move toward me.

I stood my ground, drew myself up and out, became full of myself and my own spirits.

"You will never hit me again and live." I spoke very slowly, softly. "Is this what you want to be doing when you go to meet your maker, John?"

He heard me. I watched my husband's face crumple. He slumped down on the chair and put his head in his hands.

"Don't leave me. I'm begging you. Don't go."

I walked into the bedroom and picked up the bag I'd packed that afternoon. I carried it back into the kitchen. I picked up the keys to the truck from where he'd left them on the hook beside the door.

"You take care now," I said. "I'll have Jimmy drop the truck back later." I closed the door behind me, and started walking, but I could still hear him crying. I stopped by the shed and put down a tobacco tie and some corn and seed for the rats, saying thank you. I didn't see them, but I knew they were around.

Walking to the truck was like wading through hip deep mud, but I made it. I drove down the road back to the rez and felt like I was dragging my heart all the way, tied to the back of the bumper like an old tin can.

Lauren B. Davis

Barbara's Mother's Rug

When I was thirteen, I went to a party at Barbara's house. Which was a pretty big deal for me. I wasn't a weirdo or anything, not in any specific way. Medium height, medium weight, medium face, medium bright, but I just couldn't seem to fit. I wasn't part of the group. Any group. Not that I hadn't tried enough of them.

I was the kid who ended up shuffling around hanging on the edge of things. Often on the receiving end of some stupid prank. Cayenne pepper up the nose (Come on, just *smell* this!), tent caterpillars down the blouse, or demands I do something outrageous to prove my worthiness. Eat worms or cover my shoes in dog shit. Good for a laugh but not on the "A" list as far as party invitations went.

Barbara lived a couple of streets over from me in the subdivision that had replaced the farmer's fields of a few years before. Barbara's group were new-neighbourhood kids who hadn't yet discovered my reputation for being a fifth wheel.

Barbara's parents were out for the evening and the house was filled with maybe ten or twelve teenagers. The house was awash in the too bright light specific to suburban houses of the 1960s. White walls with prints of wide-eyed children, pale blue shag carpeting, a sterility of taste. There was a crocheted dog covering the extra roll of toilet paper in the bathroom, orange and brown flowered wall-paper in the kitchen, glass topped coffee tables with chrome legs and La-z-Boy chairs with TV trays in front of them in the "rec" room.

We were listening to records and smoking cigarettes. I was feeling faintly nauseated. Cigarettes always made me feel like that and it took years of near puking to get me successfully addicted.

I didn't know this group well, and I didn't think I'd be hanging out with them for long. They seemed immature. A polished facade of maturity was my first line of defence if I sensed I'd soon be on my way out of any particular group.

Steve was a slimy little bastard. But there was a sort of salty, crusty, dick-in-your-face sex vibe coming from him. He was the kid who'd pinch your boob, or stretch out his open palm, one finger sticking up, on the seat of your chair as you sat down. Then smirk knowingly at his buddies when you shot up, shrieking. He talked, quite loudly, about getting a "woody." He was slightly feral, ferrety, weasely, and seemed always to be in total, swaggering control. He wore net T-shirts to show off what he considered impressive pecs. He seemed completely oblivious to what seemed obvious to me. He was born to end up in a checkerboard suit selling used Pintos.

Lee-Anne, on the flip side, the pack leader of the girls, had her own brand of charisma. She was tough, a tomboy, and reckless. She came from a wealthy family who lived in a big old lake front house with acres of garden all around. None of the prissy-clean rich girl ways for Lee-Anne, though. Tight corduroy pants, running shoes, sweatshirts and stringy hair were her style. She was strong and athletic and swore like a stevedore, even though she went to St. Etienne Catholic school, where the nuns, she told everybody, were afraid of her. I learned a lot of great cussing from Lee-Anne.

It was Steve who suggested the vodka. Barbara balked at first, but Lee-Anne, not to be outdone in derring-do by Weasel

Boy, took the suggestion to heart and basically bullied Barbara into acquiescence. This raiding of the parents' liquor cache was a new thing for me, and behind what I hoped was a steel cool exterior sat a bowl of lime green Jell-O. With the music of The Rolling Stones playing on the family hi-fi, out came the 40 oz., springwater-clear bottle of vodka. Blue plastic glasses were proffered to each of us, with the same implied threats no doubt later used by Jim Jones handing out glasses of spiked Kool-Aid. Not all of us fell prey to the dark influence, but I, in spite of the vague cigarette nausea, managed a healthy searing gulp.

The circle of glasses was quickly empty and I was wondering how I was going to get out of doing this again. I didn't think my stomach was going to handle another shot. Relief came when somebody asked if there was any beer. The refrigerator, kept especially for this purpose in the basement, was checked. Sure enough, it was full of Labatt's 50. Bottles were handed out. I took one, saying I liked beer better than vodka, more flavour. Right. Actually, I figured I could just nurse the bottle and nobody would be the wiser. The boys began passing the bottle of vodka back and forth, then offered it to one of the girls who had declined beer. She took a tiny lady-like swallow and passed it back to Steve.

"You call that a drink?" Steve challenged. "Typical fucking girls. Girls just can't drink like men."

"Yeah, man," said one of the Weasel Boy's pals. "Girls shouldn't even drink. Only sluts drink." This brought a round of solid agreement from the male chorus.

Lee-Anne, slouched in the bean bag char, couldn't let it pass.

"Go to hell," she countered. "You wouldn't know what to do with a slut if you found one. And since when do you consider yourself a man, Steve?" Laughter from the girls.

"You think you can drink?" said Steve, standing in front of Lee-Anne's chair, drawn up to his full height of 5'4".

"I can drink as much as you, asshole."

"Prove it."

Lee-Anne stood up slowly; she was at least two inches taller than Steve. She folded her arms across her chest.

"No problem. Go ahead. Drink up."

Had this been the Wild West of the late 1800s, no tenser stand-off could be imagined. The gunslingers squared off. The barroom went dead quiet. Somewhere in the distance a dog barked. We mere townsfolk stepped back to give 'em room.

"Ladies first," said the Testosterone Kid.

"Tell you what, you do your best, and I'll drink anything you can't finish." The bottle, it should be noted, untouched a mere twenty minutes ago, was still three-quarters full. Steve paused, eyeing the level of vodka. For the first time, he seemed unsure.

"Then I guess it's half each."

"Guess so."

"Go on, Steve!" "She's bluffing!" "She can't handle it," came the encouragement of the Kid's gang. The girls remained silent.

"I don't know about this," Barbara ventured.

"Be cool," Lee-Anne growled. "Yeah, Stevie, half each, if you can handle it. Go on."

Steve looked like his mouth might have written a check his body couldn't cash. I actually felt pity for him. I'd been there, one foot off the gangplank and nowhere to go but down. Best to retain some dignity and put on a brave face.

He put the bottle to his lips and drank, and drank, and drank some more. Then he started to cough. He turned a quite beautiful crimson shade, his eyes watered and his nose ran and he gagged. I was sure it was all going to come right back up. Everybody was laughing at him, Lee-Anne loudest of all. Somehow he managed to keep the vodka from coming out his nose. He sneezed three times. Slowly he regained his lost composure. He looked at the remaining booze in the bottle. Not even close to half gone, but still, he'd consumed a sizeable whack of alcohol. He looked woozy. He looked the colour of sea kelp. But he was on his feet.

"Shut up, you guys. She'll never beat that. Your turn." He passed the bottle to Lee-Anne.

Lee-Anne smiled and I knew just from looking at that smile there was no way she was going to be outdone. She wasn't doing it for womankind though, she was doing it for herself, for the hell of it, for the sheer pleasure of making him look like a dickless idiot. I didn't have a good feeling about this.

"That's it, Stevie? Can't even finish your half? Guess I'll have to drink yours too."

"Lee-Anne, you don't have to do this." She looked over at me, almost as surprised to hear me speak as I was.

"What do you have to do with this, Rose? Stay out of it."

She was right of course. I had nothing to do with it. I was a visitor to the party. My rank did not include permission to interfere in hierarchy rituals. People glanced over at me. I shrugged, feigning nonchalance, but they'd turned away by then. I was not note worthy.

"Bottoms up." Lee-Anne toasted the room. She raised the bottle to her mouth and poured it in. She was not so much taking swallows as just letting it flow down her throat. From the level of expertise, I was betting she'd done this before. The chanting started.

"Chug, chug, chug..."

I couldn't believe what I was seeing. The level of the bottle of harmless looking, water-coloured liquid was rapidly lowering. It was as though someone had pulled the plug in a bathtub. It slid down her gullet smooth as rain through a tin trough. I was impressed.

"Chug, chug, chug..."

There rose a mighty cheer, as the last drops of vodka disappeared. Lee-Anne raised her hands, one clasping the bottle high over her head in victory. Even Weasel Boy was impressed.

"Shit," he muttered, eyes wide.

Lee-Anne bowed to the crowd, and promptly flopped down in the beanbag chair. She accepted the congratulations of her followers with all the self-contained grace of Queen Victoria. I raised my beer bottle in recognition of the powers of a superior human being. Then I noticed the look on her face. The fighting colours were all fading away. Something was drastically amiss here.

Nobody else seemed to notice. The main event of the

evening being over, kids returned to the record player and some were starting to dance. Steve, slightly wobbly, was trying to feel up some girl in a corner and she was giggling. Barbara was trying to stop people taking any more beers and asking anybody who'd listen how she was going to explain the missing bottle of vodka to her parents.

I kept watching Lee-Anne. She tried talking to somebody now and then, trying to laugh and pretend nothing was wrong, but I could tell. The colours were just dripping out of her, leaving her ashen, beyond pale. She tried to stand up but couldn't make it and fell back into the chair. A couple of buttons popped open on her shirt. She fumbled with them, trying to get her fingers to work. She gave up. Maybe ten minutes went by before her head lolled back. Lee-Anne just lay there, her left breast showing through the opening in her blouse. The girl was gone, long gone. Passed out cold.

Steve, unmistakably snozzled himself, must have had some sort of internal boob radar.

"Titties!" he cried and stumbled over to Lee-Anne's prone form.

"Oh God," whimpered Barbara, "what's wrong with her?"

"What'd ya thick?" Steve replied. "She can't liquor her handle." His hand moved forward in the general direction of Sleeping Beauty's breast. Barbara slapped his hand away.

"Piss off! You're such a pig! Somebody help me with her."

A couple of girls went over and tried to rouse Lee-Anne. There wasn't a chance in hell she was coming around any time soon. Stevie-boy threw his arms around two of the other boys and, from the sound of the snickers, made some rather crude remarks. The girls got Lee-Anne's blouse done up again but the Leader of the Pack was down for the count. The girls wandered off and left her, half disgusted, and half admiring her nerve. I just watched. Nobody made any particular motions to include me in the little groups that were forming, but I didn't mind. At least the evening's entertainment hadn't been at my expense. I just hung around, taking the occasional sip from my Labatts' bottle, and watched Lee-Anne.

The more I watched, the more concerned I got. She was so colourless she was practically transparent. Her eyes had sunk back into her skull and she was motionless. I saw a bubble form on her lips and as she breathed it sucked back in again. A little saliva dripped out of the corner of her mouth. Ah shit, I thought, she's going to puke.

Now, I did not want to be anywhere near our Legless Leader when this event occurred. I have a weak stomach. The second I even hear anybody making even a gagging noise, it's a race to the bathroom. I stood up, planning to walk inconspicuously onto the patio.

As I strolled past the bean bag chair I glanced down at Lee-Anne. Her head was thrown way back, her mouth open. I could actually see inside her mouth. There were bits of creamy-coloured stuff in there. I could hear her breathing. I hadn't been able to hear it over the sound of the music when I was sitting across the room, but now close to her, I could. It wasn't good. She was gurgling.

I did some baby-sitting for a little girl who had seizures. Her mother told me right off that if she ever took a seizure she could vomit and I had to make sure she was lying face down so she wouldn't choke on the stuff. The little kid had never vomited under my care and for this I was profoundly grateful. Unfortunately, it looked as if the information was not going to be wasted.

"Barbara," I called, "I think we've got a problem."

"What?"

"I think Lee-Anne's sick."

"She's not sick, she's just passed out. Leave her alone."

Ah, double shit. I'd like to say the thought to just leave her there to her fate didn't even cross my mind, but it did. I wanted to just shrug my shoulders and be uninvolved. I hadn't even been hanging with this group for a month yet, and my status was still way too tenuous to be drawing any undue attention. I still had time to blend. Lee-Anne gurgled again. More bubbles. Triple shit.

I knelt down beside the chair, put one leg up on the bean bag to steady myself and the other leg on the floor. I drew a big breath. I heard someone call out.

Lauren B. Davis

"Rose, Jesus, what the fuck are you doing!?"

I grappled with Lee-Anne's inert form, hoping I would not soon be covered in bits of undigested macaroni and cheese. I held my breath. I hauled her over my leg.

Lee-Anne spewed.

The vodka ran out of her much the same way it had run in, a solid stream. A stream? Hell. This was a river, and in the river was contained, like so much flotsam, the remains of Lee-Anne's dinner. It looked like macaroni and cheese, with Spam.

"Oh, gross!"

"What the fuck!"

"My mother's new carpet!" wailed Barbara.

The carpet, I must admit, did look spectacularly revolting. Even more revolting than pale blue shag carpeting usually looks.

"She was choking," I said.

"You couldn't get a bucket first?!? What are you, nuts?! Jesus, I'm gonna get killed," said Barbara.

Lee-Anne seemed to be finished spouting vodka now and moaned. Her hands went up to her face and tried to wipe away the last of the vomit.

"Rose, you have to clean this up!"

And you know, I might have cleaned it up, if she hadn't ordered me. I surely would have helped *her* clean it up. But I just didn't want to be told to clean it up, as though I personally had puked.

"Barbara, I am not going to clean up Lee-Anne's barf. It's your house, you clean it up. I didn't barf on your carpet! She did! Christ, she could have died!"

"Don't be ridiculous! You're such a fucking drama queen! Clean it up!" Barbara stamped her foot. She actually stamped her foot.

"Fush off," said Lee-Anne, to no one in particular.

"No," I said, to Barbara.

Well, I figured right then and there that I had worn out my welcome with my companions of recent weeks.

"Get out," said Barbara. "You bitch, get out! Nobody wants you here." And as no one spoke up to deny this, I assumed it to be true.

26

So, leaving them to clean up, I went home. And yes, I cried. But it was as much out of a sense of terrible injustice as hurt.

I saw Lee-Anne hanging around outside our school a couple of days later. She skipped out of her school a lot and would stand around chain smoking in our parking lot. I never could figure out why that was better than staying at the Catholic school. I half expected her to say thanks, or at least acknowledge what had happened. It was just the two of us, after all, with no one else to hear.

She stared at me.

"I hear you made me puke the other night."

"You were choking," I said.

"Lighten up, for Christ's sake." She snorted out a cloud of smoke.

For the tiniest, briefest nanosecond, I thought I saw Lee-Anne's eyes flick down to the ground. Just for a second, I thought I saw her drop her eyes. Then she raised her head and spit through her teeth. The slimy oyster wad landed on the hood of Miss Craig, the Phys. Ed. teacher's, turd-brown hatchback.

"Poor old Rose, you just don't get it, do you?"

"Nope, I guess I just don't get it."

"Live fast, die young, and leave a good looking corpse behind. Words of wisdom, kiddo." She put her cigarette back in her mouth and let it dangle from her chapped lower lip. She pushed her red gloveless hands into the pockets of her imitation leather jacket and stared at the leaf-bare trees, wind-tears forming in the corners of her eyes.

I turned and went back into class, leaving Lee-Anne leaning up against the side of the red brick building. She blew smoke rings. Caught by the wind gusts, they blew apart to nothing in the cold November air.

Lauren B. Davis

Drop In Any Time

Word of what happened to Stewart circulated quickly. *Did you hear? Did you hear? Did you hear?* The story swept through the streets like water in the gutter.

The Toronto neighbourhood was one of oak-lined streets and second hand bookstores, coffee shops and bars with tiny spaces called "open stages" where on Friday or Sunday night anyone could read poetry, rant about the conservative provincial government or sing the song they'd just written.

Stewart knew every shopkeeper by name, knew how many kids each had, was recognised by every panhandler; plus Elio, the guy who ran the news-stand, depended on him to drop off a hot coffee every day on his way home from work. Stewart was a neighbourhood fixture, an always-smiling face. He was kind, and so if people made jokes about his bad comb-over or his brightly patterned vests, or his sometimes overpowering aftershave, they never teased him to his face. He was also, if the truth be told, a bit of a gossip. If you wanted to know anything about anyone in the neighbourhood, Stewart was the man to see. He knew where Mrs. Cheung's daughter was hiding out when she ran away from home, and why. He knew the amount Mr. Davidson had to pay when he was audited last year and why the Campbells' marriage broke up. He even knew the name of the girlfriend.

Every Sunday morning Stewart went to the Renaissance café for a vegetarian brunch. There he met with four or five friends and they talked over each other's romantic problems, job problems, talked about the books they'd just read or were attempting to write, the politics that influenced them. He was the sort of fellow who made friends with strangers at the next table, drew them into conversation and later exchanged phone numbers.

He worked in the printing department of the University of Toronto, copying reports and dissertations, brochures and lesson outlines. The job paid the rent. But he knew he was far more sophisticated than his career indicated. His real interest lay the healing powers of music and one day he dreamed of travelling to Mongolia to study shamanic chants.

"I've never heard of a sickness or an injury that could not be made better by listening to Vivaldi's Four Seasons," he said. "You can laugh, but just try it the next time you get a bad cold."

On a day in June, warm enough that you could finally do without a jacket, Stewart stood in line to pay for his *Globe and Mail* and noticed a boy standing behind him. He was eighteen or nineteen, tall and lanky, dressed like a million other kids his age: running shoes, jeans, a T-shirt that read "There's no such thing as gravity, the earth just sucks." He wore a gold ring through the right side of his lower lip.

"The news just keeps getting worse and worse, doesn't it? Just for once I'd like to see something in the paper about someone *not* doing something despicable to someone else, wouldn't you?" said Stewart.

"Yeah, I guess. What a world, eh?"

That was pretty much the extent of the conversation, but it was enough to make them remember each other the next time they passed in the street and Stewart said hello. The kid asked

Stewart if he could spare any change. Stewart gave him a couple of "loonies" and introduced himself. The kid said his name was Philip.

And so it went. Stewart and Philip met in the street, turning the corner, in the convenience store, in the donut shop on Bloor and St. George. Once or twice they struck up a conversation. Stewart bought Philip cups of coffee, heard about his troubles. He had that knack. People he barely knew were always telling him their troubles.

Philip told Stewart how hard it was to make ends meet, to pay the rent on the room he shared with his girlfriend, Pam. Philip said he'd had to sell his stereo, his guitar. He was looking for work, he said. Stewart sympathised. Times were hard. Now and then he slipped the kid twenty bucks, bought him a hamburger, or gave him a few dollars for bus tokens, just to help out. He liked Philip, felt a soft spot for the kid. He wanted to do what he could to make his life a little easier until his situation improved.

Once he invited Philip to eat at his apartment. The kid sat hunched over his pasta, fiddling with the ring in his lip, the pierced hole red and inflamed, slightly crusted with infection. It made Stewart a little queasy to watch, and he spent the time focused on fussing about the tiny kitchen. Philip seemed ill at ease, looking around constantly and shifting in his seat. Stewart put this down to Philip's embarrassment with his own reduced circumstances. He concluded this was why he'd never learned where Philip lived - because it would make him uncomfortable to have Stewart see his dingy lodgings.

Late one sticky Friday night in early August, it was after 11:00, there was a knock at the door. Stewart was reading, thinking about how good it would feel to soon be tucked up in bed. He went to the door, expecting it to be Craig, one of his neighbours, who locked himself out with regularity and left a key at Stewart's. He opened the door. There stood Philip, smiling, and behind him another man and a young woman, her hair dyed a gothic blue-black.

"Philip! What a surprise! What's up?"

Philip moved toward him, causing him to step back into the

room. The other two followed close behind. Now they were all standing inside Stewart's apartment. The other man closed the door and leaned up against it. Philip twirled the ring in his lip. He was standing too close to Stewart. Stewart backed up another step, smelling beer, cigarettes and sweat.

"Are you all right? Is something wrong?" said Stewart. When Stewart's friends showed up this late at night, something was usually wrong; a romantic break-up, a sick relative, something Stewart could be helpful with. Something a cup of tea and a long chat could help solve.

He wished Philip would say something.

"Is this Pamela?" Stewart extended his arm to shake the girl's hand. Her skin was very pale, her lipstick and fingernails painted a grape colour so dark it looked almost black. She didn't take his hand. He dropped it. He looked at Philip.

"Philip?"

"Stewart, man, we've come to get your stereo."

"My stereo," Stewart repeated, "...you want my stereo?"

"Clever boy."

Stewart thought Philip's eyes looked very odd, hollow and colourless, like mine shafts.

"Philip, be serious!" Stewart tried out a little laugh. "My stereo. Very funny." He waited for Philip to join in on the joke, but Philip remained mute. Stewart concluded the situation required normalcy.

"Why don't we have a cup of coffee? We can sit down and talk about what's going on. You're always welcome here. You know that. I told you to drop by any time. Now, I know you don't really want my stereo. I mean, it's so silly. Do you want a coffee?" Stewart felt like a fool, prattling on this way, but he couldn't seem to stop.

Philip turned to his companions. "You guys want a fucking coffee?"

The man, who was shorter than Philip, wider, and sported a variety of tattoos, one of a spider on his left cheek, said, "Coffee, sure. Why the fuck not?" He rubbed his hand over his shaved head a couple of times.

32

"Let's have a tea party!" he yelled, and the two young men laughed.

The girl stood staring at Philip, her hands stuffed in the over-size men's coat she wore.

"OK, Stew. Why don't you scamper into the kitchen and fix us a nice cup of hot coffee."

Stewart felt he should really ask them to leave, but now that he'd offered them coffee and they'd accepted, he didn't see how he could. They would probably just leave after the coffee. He could keep the situation under control. If he just stayed calm and didn't let on he was frightened, he'd be OK. There really was nothing to be afraid of, it was simply that the hour was late and Philip was making jokes in bad taste. But young people did things differently. Philip wouldn't hurt him. Philip was a friend. In an hour Stewart would be in bed, safe and amused at how nervous he'd been.

In the kitchen he hurried about, boiling the kettle, spooning instant coffee into mugs, grabbing milk from the refrigerator, sugar, putting things on a tray. This is going to be OK, he kept repeating, like a mantra. This is going to be OK. OK. OK. He didn't want to leave them alone in the living room. He heard noises, not talking, but scuffling noises. Metallic noises. He couldn't hear voices and that made him more uncomfortable. He picked up the tray and walked back into the living room. As he came through the doorway he could see Philip and the Spider Man. They were dismantling the stereo. The speakers were already unwired, placed by the door. Philip was bending over the back of the stereo casing, fiddling with the wires. Spider Man was hunched behind the equipment. Stewart couldn't see the Gothic girl.

"Stop it! Philip! Don't..."

Before he could finish the sentence he felt the back of his head explode in a starburst of yellow and red lights. He dropped the tray and fell forward to his knees in the broken china and spilled coffee. He tried to turn and see what had hit him. Gothic Girl stood behind him. She had a hammer in her right hand. That hand was raising itself up again. And coming down.

"Don't," Stewart whispered.

But she did.

The first sense Stewart regained was sound. Medium-sized sounds, like big rodents moving around the room. He couldn't understand. Pigeons on the roof. Then the pain began. His head hurt, his jaw hurt. His jaw felt like someone had put a white-hot ice pick in the joint. His mouth was open. Close it. The pain would stop if he closed his mouth. He couldn't. He had something in his mouth. He opened his eyes. *Oh God*.

Stewart was tied to one of his dining room chairs. His ankles were tied to the legs of the chair. His arms were tied to the arms of the chair. His chest was tied to the back of the chair. He had something stuffed in his mouth and something tied around his head holding it in. It was hard to breathe. His head hurt. A lot. He was dizzy. He was nauseated. He was afraid he'd throw up, choke to death. He had to stay calm. He wanted to cry.

He heard noises from the bedroom.

Philip and Spider Man had the stereo packed up and ready to go. They also had his wallet, his watch and his silver candlesticks on the table. There was a pillowcase next to the door that looked as though it had some things in it. He didn't have much else of any monetary value. No television. He couldn't imagine what would be in the pillowcase. Why didn't they just go now?

Gothic Girl came out of the kitchen and looked at him. She had no expression on her face. It was as though, under the white make-up, there was nothing, just empty air, the paint merely giving form to the void. She walked into the bedroom. A moment later she came back out, followed by Philip and Spider Man.

"Weren't sure you'd come back to us, man. But glad you aren't going to miss the rest of the party." Philip smiled. Spider Man smiled. "Why don't you put the kettle on again, Babe. We didn't get our coffee."

Gothic Girl went back to the kitchen. There was something obscene about this parody of domestic roles. It was perverse. The girl appeared back at the door from the kitchen. She had the electric kettle in her hand. She stooped down and put it on the floor next to his chair. She plugged it in. Stewart didn't understand. Why would she not just make coffee in the kitchen? He was missing something, his brain addled by pain and fear. There was something he was supposed to know.

The kettle began to boil. She unplugged it. She stood up with it in her hand and raised it over his head.

Losing consciousness took some time. He was more grateful for that state of oblivion than he had been for anything in his life. By that point he was past hoping they would stop torturing him, past praying someone would sense what was going on in his apartment and call the police, past imploring behind his gag for mercy. He just wanted to faint.

He had wondered from time to time, when listening to ghastly news reports of atrocities committed in far off lands, if he would break under torture and tell his captors what they wanted to know. Now he knew the answer to that question. *Of course he would.* The horror of this particular situation was that there was nothing they wanted to know. They just wanted to keep doing what they were doing until they didn't want to do it anymore. It was quite simple, really. The only thing required of him was to continue feeling and he did that very well, until eventually, a merciful God granted the reprieve, the pardon, of insensibility.

When he came to, he was alone.

He lay on the floor. His ankles were still tied to the chair, although his hands had been freed. This struck him as funny, that his tormentors had been thoughtful enough to untie his hands. He couldn't imagine why. He giggled and another part of his psyche, far off and away somewhere, thought, *Oh dear, laughing can't be a good sign. I might be going crazy.*

His brain worked mechanically, taking in details, without emotion, as though some vital wire had been disconnected.

His skin was sticky. He was covered with a mixture of blood, mucous, peeling skin, egg shells, green paint, cigarette butts and other things he had trouble identifying.

He was extremely tired. His body was lead, although he didn't feel very much pain, for which he was immensely grateful. He concluded the best thing he could do was sleep. That seemed very sensible.

Lauren B. Davis

He untied his ankles and crawled to the couch. He hauled himself up onto the soft cool leather and instantly fell asleep.

Craig, the neighbour who often locked himself out, found Stewart later in the morning. First he was sick to his stomach, and then he called an ambulance, and so Stewart did not die, although he wished for some time afterward that he had.

His friends David and Diane came by the hospital to visit. They brought a Walkman and Vivaldi tapes.

"We thought this might help," they said, softly, awed by the presence of so much equipment, so many blinking lights and bleeping monitors. They put the tape in, and placed earphones gently on the batting of the bandages, trying not to hurt him.

"That's very kind of you," he said, although his words were hard to understand given the condition of his mouth.

When his friends left he buzzed for the nurse and asked her to disconnect the music.

Stewart moved away some months later, when he was released from hospital. He didn't keep in touch, although he was polite when anyone called round to see how he was doing. He said the therapy was helping.

When he was gone, and the twitter of talk died down, the neighbourhood was a quieter place than it had been. More reserved. More self-conscious. The "perpetrators" had never been caught. They were still out there somewhere. People drew their blinds and checked their locks twice before turning in. New people moved in and found this neighbourhood no different than other sections of the city, no warmer, no more welcoming. They wondered why their friends had raved about it. People hesitated before unfamiliar faces. They didn't strike up conversations over their morning cappuccinos. After all, you never could tell, could you? The world was such a dangerous place these days.

Change of Season

"How, in the name of Heaven, do people bear it?" thought Caroline Edgeweather. It was intolerable. She hunched deeper over her desk in a protective effort to block out the sound of the chain saw which had been chewing its way through the tree limbs outside her house for the past forty-five minutes. It was no use. She might as well be in a dentist's chair for the way the sound bore into her skull. She would never get the chapter finished with this satanic racket shaking loose the fillings in her teeth.

Caroline admitted the tree pruning needed to be done. The trees had been sadly neglected in the previous year. The shrubs the same. And the hedges and the rose bushes looked like Medusa's hair. This work was necessary. She had called the gardener herself. But God, the sound was torturous, cruel, un-relenting.

Caroline had been sensitive to noise all her life, and the older she got the worse the sensitivity became. As a child her mother said Caroline used to run out of the room with her hands clamped over her ears every time the vacuum cleaner was turned on. Now, at forty-eight, everything irritated her, from the

Parkers' shrill giggle-shrieking three-year-old, to Molson, the Windsors' barking golden retriever, to the incessant **kachung, kachung, thoop, whackity, whackity** dribbling of sixteen-year-old Dennis Windsors' basketball. It was a sport in which she had once hoped the teenager would lose interest. Annoyingly enough though, he seemed only more obsessed with the orange ball and hoop each time the afternoon sun spotlighted the small asphalt patch directly below her office window. *Demon-child*, thought Caroline, *why can't he smoke grass and vegetate in front of computer games like other teenagers?*

Her sister said her increasing crotchety nature was the result of menopause and went on to say it would only get worse before it got better, if it ever did. Caroline suspected something no more sinister than a well-developed neurosis. Naomi had been having her own hot flashes and mood swings for ten years. Misery loved company.

Brrrrraaaaaaaah, brrrrraaaaaah, brrrrrraaaaaaAAAHHHH! The chain saw belched forth.

Why did it seem to be one of the universe's immutable laws that noise was produced in direct proportion to her need for quiet? It never failed to build to a deafening crescendo in the middle of hours when she did her best work. Would it violate some unspoken contract between the devil and the book critics if workmen came in the morning, a time relegated to correspondence and reviewing her scribbled notes? Either of these activities she would gladly forsake. But no, all noise-makers in the neighbourhood insisted on cranking up their diabolically deafening activity of choice just as she prepared to work. And, now that she thought about it, she was sure she had requested Daniel come on Wednesday, if he must come in the afternoon, as Wednesday was the day Marie, the cleaning lady, was also in the house and Caroline was already resigned to doing minimal work.

Brrrrraaaaaaah, brrrrrrraaaaaaah, brrrraa, braaa, brRRRRAAAACGH!

Now she was going to miss two afternoons' worth of work, at least, as she doubted Daniel would be finished in one day. The gardens were too extensive and too badly neglected. They had become this neglected, of course, because she couldn't bear this sort of hullabaloo on a regular basis.

Brrrrraaaaaah, brrrrrrraaaaaah, brrrraa, braaa, brRRRRAAAACGH!

It sounded like an enormous mechanical chicken with a wrench in its gullet.

Surely, if she concentrated, she'd be able to work through this. Other people did. Other people, in fact, seemed almost immune to noise pollution. They slept on aeroplanes crowded with whining five-year-olds, they read in public places, they relaxed on body-bloated beaches, lived calm lives, oblivious to trucks, early morning birds and late night motorcycles, all of which sent Caroline into fits of irritation.

But she was determined now. She would get at least the next three pages written, chain saw or no chain saw. She pulled her old grey cardigan, her ritual writing garment, tighter around her middle. *Right*, she thought, *here we go. Fall into the page. Allow yourself to disappear into the eternal place of endeavour. Mind over chain saw.* She read over the last two sentences and tried to capture the sense of where she had been going, the mood of the piece...

BRRRRRAAAAAAAAAAHHHH, BRRRAAAAhhhhh, brrrrrrrrAAAAH!

"Bloody, bloody, bloody HELL," she said out loud to the sound-filled room. "This is impossible! Impossible!" She felt as though she had been flayed, all her raw nerve endings exposed to the violently vibrating air. She slammed her pen down on the table, nearly overturning her coffee cup. She rose and stormed out of the room, down the stairs and across the hall to the front door.

She would scream at the young man in the tree, hurl abuse at him, scald him with her words, sear his eyebrows right off his skull, tell him to take his bloody noise machine and bugger off! Damn the garden! It would feel good to do this! Let the trees go to hell. She flung open the door, marched out onto the porch, hands on her hips, feet in a wide flat-footed stance. All she needed to complete the picture of herself as frontiers-woman protecting the homestead from outlaws was a rifle. She looked up in the tree, shading her eyes from the blinding sun.

"Young man! Daniel Cummings! Daniel! Turn that infernal machine off this instant!"

He looked down from his perch and waved. Grinning idiotically, he couldn't hear a word. She gestured frantically. She stuck her fingers in her ears, her mouth a wide-drawn grimace. She slashed at her throat. She pointed at the evil machine. Daniel Cummings looked at her as though she was quite mad, then laughed, bowing his head, as he understood and pointed a finger skyward. He shut the machine off. The comparative silence was so great Caroline imagined every tiny worm, sparrow and grub in the garden must be breathing a sigh of relief.

"Hi, Miss Edgeweather, how ya doin'? Great fall we're having isn't it? Bit cold though, gonna be an early winter, I'd bet," said Daniel.

He grinned a huge crooked grin at her and looked just as his father had done, all those years ago, a lock of sandy hair falling over his eyes, his beautifully muscled arms and thighs stretching at the fabric of his work clothes.

"How's the next book coming? Last one sure was a doozey. Dad read it twice you know."

"Well, yes, I'm glad you all liked it."

"Sure did, yup, sure did." My God, he was the spitting image of his father, with his same slow way of talking, the almost cowboy-like inflections to his speech, the old fashioned mannerisms.

"You are making an ungodly racket you know."

"Yes ma'am, I guess I am. But you've got a beautiful garden here. Shame to let it go down this way. Woman such as yourself deserves to live in beauty."

Damn the poetic soul of the men in that family, she thought.

"Daniel, I was wondering..." she said, intending to tell him to forget it, just forget it, let the garden grow up like Sleeping Beauty's barrier against the world.

"Yes ma'am?"

Oh bother it! She couldn't bring herself to blast him with

that loopy grin plastered on his face. Not when it brought out the adorable familiar lines framing his mouth like parentheses. Damn. She sighed and resigned herself to losing a day's work. She might as well admit it: there was no fool like a middle-aged writer.

"Would you like a cup of tea?"

"I surely would ma'am, that's awful kind of you. Thanks, Miss Edgeweather."

"Five minutes. Come down from that tree and give us all a break."

Caroline retraced her steps into the house to the sound of the chain saw starting up again. In the kitchen she put the kettle on the stove and delicately removed cups and saucers from the cupboards, trying not to add to the clamour. She turned the radio up loud to try to drown out the sound, but this only annoyed her more and so she shut it off.

She waited for the kettle to boil and moved home-made shortbread around on a blue and white china plate. She shouldn't ask Daniel in. That would only delay his departure and as it was he'd doubtless be there for hours. But it was too cold to sit outside. And he was working hard. He deserved a cup of tea.

She walked into the washroom beside the kitchen and looked in the mirror. Nearly fifty. But not so bad. Blessed by a rose-petal complexion and dark hair, with silver streaks that looked dramatic rather than dowdy. She ran her hand over her throat. Yes, well, there was a little crêpe there. You couldn't hide it but she'd be damned if she'd go under the knife. End up with all the same wrinkles, only pulled up instead of down, with a smile that looked as though one was caught in an astronaut's g-force. She turned sideways and smoothed the front of her skirt. Still flat. Firm. For a woman her age.

The kettle's whistle called her back to the kitchen.

She went to the door and signalled Daniel he should come down.

He tromped his boots on the back step, shaking off as much dirt as possible, and stepped across the threshold. He took off his jean jacket and she indicated he could hang it on a hook in the hall.

Lauren B. Davis

"Mind if I wash up a bit?" he said, and held out his wide, strong-fingered hands to illustrate the need.

"On your left," she said. "Soap's next to the sink, and a towel."

She sat at the table and stirred the tea leaves in the pot, settled the tea cosy, letting it steep to a rich flavour. He opened the bathroom door and came into the kitchen. He'd washed his face and strands of his hair dangled dark and wet in front of his brown eyes. He pushed them back with both hands. Caroline couldn't help but notice the perfect triangle of his torso. He threw a leg over the chair to her left, and sat. The table was pushed into the corner of the room. There were only two chairs.

Caroline poured the tea.

"Sugar? Milk?"

"Just sugar, thanks." She passed him the sugar bowl. He put three teaspoons in his cup. His father had liked his tea strong and sweet, too.

"So tell me Daniel, what sort of shape do you think my poor old garden's really in? Is there any hope?"

"There's always hope, Miss E. And it's not so bad. Just been left alone a bit too long is all. Nothing we can't put back right as rain. You did the right thing to call. Another season and I can't say what might be. But I won't let that happen." The cup looked small and fragile in his hand.

"Do you want a mug, instead of that cup? It's been a while since a man was in this kitchen. I didn't think."

"Naw, that's just fine. I promise I won't break it." He grinned, and Caroline grinned back.

"Cookie?" she said, and held out the plate to him.

"You make them yourself?"

"I can't abide store-bought baked goods."

He put a cookie in his mouth and bit. It was butter-rich and light. Several crumbs stuck to his lip and a few more fell to his lap. He leaned over the plate. Her hand came up, without her having directed it to do so, and was on its way to brush softly at his mouth. She caught herself and pulled the errant hand to her ear lobe, as though adjusting her earring. Daniel brushed the

42

crumbs from his lap into his palm and dropped them onto the plate.

His father had been partial to her lemon cake and home-made bread, filled with plump raisins and cinnamon. She remembered how his mouth had worked as he chewed, his tongue flicking out now and then, loath to let even the tiniest morsel escape. There had been an afternoon involving her raspberry jam. It had started with scones over tea and ended up in the big old claw-foot bathtub.

Yes, Ethan Cummings had been fond of bread and cake and jam. Dan Dickson, the mechanic at Ed's Garage, where she'd been taking her battered old army jeep for years, had loved her apricot tart, the one with almonds in the crust. And Joshua Cary, meter man, couldn't get enough of her walnut brownies.

She'd been known all over town for her baking. Ethan's son was a cookie man. Caroline could tell.

"Have another one," she said. He took one and said thanks.

"You should think about what you want to do with the Bishop's Weed," he went on. "It's a pretty plant and all, with them Queen Anne-type flowers, but it'll creep into everything. I tell people that even though they bloom for a long time, they should resist the temptation, 'cause they're harder than hell to keep in line. Make good ground cover - about two miles off. I'd recommend you let me pull it all out and replace it with something more manageable." Daniel leaned forward, putting his weight on his forearms.

"Whatever you say." His youth was appealing. His skin was so smooth, so sun-blessed. He moved with none of the hesitant stiffness of an older man. She felt warm and sticky as honey between her thighs. A second pulse began to throb there.

"How old are you now, Daniel?"

"Turned twenty-two last February."

"Tell me, are you happy now that you'll be taking over your Dad's company?"

"He's still running things, with Mom 'a course, but I do most of the heavy work now."

"You're certainly strong enough for it. Look at the arms on

you!"

He flexed his right arm, forming a muscle that threatened to burst the seams of his flannel plaid work shirt.

"Don't need no gym to stay in shape when you're a working man."

"I should say not. You must be beating off the girls with a stick."

"Well, I do all right," he shook his head, in a modest way. "Been seeing a little of Charlene Mitchell."

"Charlene. Well, she's a nice little girl. Is it serious?"

"I don't know. Serious? I might be a bit too young for serious. But I like her a lot."

"And I'm sure she likes you. Is she good to you?"

"She treats me right."

"She's a wise girl then. I bet it takes a lot to keep a man like you happy. Almost more than one little girl could do." She smiled at him as she stretched, arching her back and letting her sweater pull taunt across her breasts. Her breasts were still good, more voluptuous now than when she'd been young. Age had its compensations.

"Ma'am?"

"Oh, you know what I mean Daniel. I may never have married, but that doesn't mean I'm completely innocent, you know."

Daniel picked up his cup and drained the last of the tea.

"Have some more," she said, picking up the teapot, feeling confident that the afternoon wouldn't be a total waste. He surprised her by standing up.

"I better get back to work now. I've got a schedule to keep to."

"I won't mind if you fall a little behind."

"Well, Miss Edgeweather, I'll tell you," he looked down at his boots, stuffed his hands in his pockets, "I've been given pretty strict instructions from my Ma not to dawdle about here. Got other clients I got to see this afternoon."

Caroline walked toward him.

"Aren't you a little old to be listening to everything your Mama tells you?" she said. She stood close enough to him that she had to tilt her head up to look at him, and could feel the heat of his skin. Daniel's pupils were dilated and his breathing was audible.

"Yes Ma'am, maybe I am, but even my Daddy says that when it comes to some subjects, my Mom just knows best." Caroline stepped back. She picked up her cup and plate, brought them to the sink. "I believe this might be one of those subjects. Keeping to a schedule. You wouldn't want our clients to be left unsatisfied, would you?"

She kept her back to him.

"Certainly not. We wouldn't want that."

"Well, I'll get on with it then. And I'll tell Dad you said hello, shall I? Tell him you're still a mighty, mighty fine cook."

He closed the door gently behind him. Caroline cleaned the table. She couldn't abide an untidy kitchen. She was halfway to the sink, carrying the teapot, his teacup and saucer, balanced on the plate, when the chain saw began again.

Brrrrraaaaaaaah,brrrrraaaaaah, brrrrrrrrraaaaaaaaAAAHHHH!

The sound startled her and she jumped. She cup leapt off the saucer and smashed on the floor.

"Damn it! Damn it to hell!" she yelled. She looked at the pieces of yellow and green china, pieces too tiny to glue together, and felt tears well up. It had been an old cup, one of her mother's, and it was a favourite. Part of a time long past, well worked, pretty in an old fashioned way. All those years, and she had to be the one to break it. She hated breaking things, hated to see the end of something that had withstood decades of life. She angrily swept up the jagged pieces, wiping at her eyes. The noise from the garden washed over her like the swell of a malevolent wave. She clamped her mouth shut, afraid at any second she might start screaming.

Lauren B. Davis

Strays

Everyone said the change of scene would do Janet good. After what had happened. After her great loss. After what cousin Kendra of the crystals and tarot cards referred to as her "spiritual amputation." Any other kind of death could be spoken of directly. But not this kind.

"Think of it as medicinal," Kendra said. "A healing journey."

"Just what the doctor ordered," said her husband Ian.

"Take your time, don't worry about how long it takes. Your job will wait," said her boss, clearing his throat, uncomfortable, wanting to get off the phone quickly.

"What are you afraid of?" said her psychiatrist.

She was worn down. Maybe they were right. A trip might be what she needed. Medicinal in fact.

They packed bags. They stopped the mail. They brought the cat to his mother's. They landed in Spain, the land of passion, pleasure and a sunny warm respite after Oregon's gloomy February.

But the medicine wasn't working. The spoon of travel was at her lips, but she couldn't swallow. She still felt like half of her was missing.

The little village outside Cadiz, where they started their trip, had been a disappointment. What had been described as a dilapidated fishing village, conjuring up images of quaint tilted houses, weather-worn faces and men repairing nets in the harbour, turned out to be dilapidated indeed, but as only an industrial zone suffering from unemployment can be.

The mattress in the hotel had been damp, the room dark. The corridors of the converted monastery were stone and tile, and the footsteps of the hotel staff echoed day and night like the ghosts of booted dancers. Ian slept like a log, any time of the day or night, in any place. Janet's body would not adjust to the hours the Spanish kept. She was someone who liked to be in bed at 10:00 and up at dawn. In Spain, life arrives at the side of your table at midnight or later and Janet felt out of sync.

She stood in front of the bathroom mirror one morning, her bare feet icy on the stone floor. She looked unhappily at herself. Her eyes were pinkish, her skin mottled and scrunched from a twisted sleep. These days she avoided most reflective surfaces. They reminded her too sharply of that other familiar face, now lost forever. It always surprised her, that quick prick of misunderstanding, and she had grown to resent her own face, its lines and planes and rounded cheeks. What good was a face that could never simply be itself, but must always be, as well, a ghost face?

She brushed her teeth and rinsed her mouth, ran a comb through her hair, put a dab of lip-gloss on her mouth, all without looking at herself again. She doubted this attempt at fixing up did much good, but neither would it do any good to crumble here. She closed her eyes and tried to visualise a gentle sea with golden sunlight and frolicking dolphins, as Kendra had suggested during times of stress. She failed.

"Fuck it," she said, watching the water swirl down the drain.

She walked to the terrace, where Ian stood looking at the orange groves on the hillsides.

"I will *never* get used to the hours the Spanish keep - dinner at midnight, sleeping at noon. I feel like a robin living in a world run by bats," she said. Ian laughed.

"That's my girl," he said, and put his arm around her. She willed herself to stay still, not pull away.

They drove themselves to remain awake one night, until some small hour in the morning when, a waiter had told them, the flamenco would begin in a tiny cubby-hole of a bar down the street from their hotel. The room was filled with elderly people, smoking dark cigarettes and drinking coffee or wine with fruit floating in it. Two young women in matching turquoise dresses began to dance on the minuscule stage and for a while, Janet and Ian were transfixed. It was clear these elderly men and women seated at the table around them were not simply the audience, but judges as well. Their periodic clapping encouraged the girls; their silence criticised them.

One of the girls was more voluptuous, with firm curves straining at the fabric across her breasts and hips, the arch in her back accentuating the smallness of her waist. Next to her the other looked like a child and no matter how winning her movements, it was the girl with the lushness to her who mesmerised. She held her head as though it were a prize to be offered only to someone worthy, and kicked aside the flounced train of her dress like an unwanted suitor. The girls danced in tandem, presenting themselves and then denying, displaying themselves and then jumping back, as though just out of reach of the hands of men, or the horns of bulls.

When they returned to their musty room, Janet confessed the dancing and the implications of the movements had aroused her, and Ian was relieved. He made love to her, on the damp mattress. But she held on to him too tightly, and cried afterward, turning her face to the pillow as he rubbed her back.

All through the days, she was a mess of porous clay, the opening in her heart sucking up all sorts of impressions from Spain. But she seemed unable to find her own balance, her own stability. Ian's hand, kneading the back of her neck, only annoyed her. She knew he wanted to help, to soothe, but the gesture only served to remind her of her fragile status. *Stop hovering, she said. Stop fussing over me.* And he did, but still he watched her from the sides of his eyes, being solicitous even by trying not to be solicitous. She tried not to be so sensitive.

Still, even with the kaleidoscope of psychic flashes, Spain was a mystery to her. The landscape was not as she had expected. She had thought to find fecund hills covered with orange groves and luxuriant vine-covered arbours. What they encountered as they drove in their small, somewhat battered, rental car was a sun-blasted landscape, unforgiving and unyielding, rocky and stern. Janet felt sorrow as they drove and once, between Seville and Granada, broke into tears. She told Ian she found the land unbearably sad.

"It's like the land is grieving something," she said, "like all that bullfight stuff, the metaphors of blood and sand. It's as though it were connected."

Ian gripped the wheel a little tighter, drove a little faster. She knew she wasn't making sense, but she felt as though the legends built on death and violence were crowding in on her.

"Maybe we should have gone to Ireland," he said. "Maybe that would have been better. Soft rain and sheep fields."

"Bodhrans and penny whistles," she said.

"If Spain's making things worse, we could leave. Go to Ireland, go anywhere you want."

"No." She dried her eyes, touched the back of his neck. "I'll be fine. I promise."

"It's not about where we are, Jan, it's about how you feel."

"I'll be fine."

They arrived in Granada. The landscape became gentler and greener; the land no longer looked as though its bones were showing through broken skin. Their hotel was on the hill near the Alhambra. It was decorated in the Moorish fashion, full of brass-topped tables and tiled floors, a heavy wooden bedstead and an enormous bath, which, although it didn't work properly, was lovely to look at. They had tea on the terrace and ate oranges. Ian wrote postcards to his family as Janet read a guidebook. She learned of gypsy caves just on the outskirts of the city, in the Sacromonet hills, and thought they should go there. She wanted to get up and away somewhere, into the air, into someplace freer and less constricted by buildings. She thought the ancient liberty of the caves would be healing.

For Ian's sake she vowed to be gay, not to be irritated by the noise in the streets, unclean rest rooms and greasy food. He was unaffected by such things. He wanted them to soak in the atmosphere, the food and the music. He wanted her to relax, to be better. He was untroubled by stomach problems or jet lag. He indulged her finicky gut, her somewhat prissy concern over bacteria, her sensitivity to noise of all kinds.

The next day they set out for the caves, to walk there, taking advantage of the warm morning sun. Hand in hand they climbed down the long flights of stairs leading from the hotel's eagle perch on the side of the mountain, down into the city, stopping to take photos in the gaping windows of half ruined houses, or beside low stone walls covered with bougainvillaea. They planned to cross through the urban streets to the older section of the city beyond and finally up to the hills themselves.

The way was unpleasant. Scaffolds blocked the narrow sidewalks and jack hammers slapped noise into their faces and dust into their pores. Traffic was full of diesel fumes and car horns. The intersections were confusing and Janet was afraid each time they stepped off a curb they'd be hit by speeding cars. She began to feel the strange porous feeling again, as though she were ingesting all the impressions of the lives around her, without words, just sensations of longing, or sorrow, or of rage. Never did she feel joy at these moments, never serenity. She simply felt overcome by the atmosphere of the lives of others. She could not control it, could only grit her teeth until it passed.

She pressed her lips into a firm line, breathed deeply and pushed on through the city streets. Past stores selling guitars and leather purses, furniture and brightly painted fans, brass figures of matadors and bulls with swords sticking out from their backs. When Ian lagged behind, stopping to look at postcards or small wooden boxes with mother-of-pearl inlay, she could have screamed, he was so slow, so meandering. Untroubled by the chaos all around him. It was maddening. She said nothing and tried to smile and to be patient.

They passed through the chaotic bowl of the city and finally began to climb again, up toward the third of the three hills. The streets were less busy here, quieter and blessedly free of the sounds of construction. Janet began to relax, slowing her own pace and stopping now and then to look in shop windows.

Soon they passed out of the city proper and found themselves in an area clearly in the midst of some sort of housing boom. A subdivision, not unlike those they were familiar with back in America, was being built, although for some reason, there were no workmen. Foundations gaped in the dusty earth and reinforcing rods jutted up out of the concrete, looking dangerous and rusty. Ian found this evidence of economic growth encouraging. He liked the bustle of financial improvement. He was fond of progress in its most material incarnations. Janet felt ill at ease. The place looked to her as though it was caving in, rather than going up. It looked like the aftermath of war, rather than the inception of prosperity.

"Are you sure we're going the right way?" she asked.

"Yes, I think so. Look at the map." Ian pulled it out of his back pocket and rustled it open.

"See, we're here, at least I think we are. That's the hotel up there, and over to the right of us should be the caves. I can't really see on the map where all this construction is; it's too new. But it must be here," he pointed to a place on the map, "this blank area. If we go through those fields, we should come out near the caves. There's even a path, so we can't be the first to come this way."

"You know, the guy at the hotel said drug users live in the caves."

"I'm sure it's safe. I mean, maybe not at night in the summer, when all of Europe is swamped with backpacking druggies, but in February? It's safe." He smiled his big toothy grin at her, goofy and reassuring.

"We'll just walk for a bit. What's the worst that can happen? We end up somewhere interesting, or we won't and we'll come back. You game?"

"I guess so," she said.

"Well, all right then." Ian set out resolutely across the fields, empty except for the rocks and flotsam of plastic bags, discarded rusty cans and bits of broken glass. Janet followed.

They had walked for just a few minutes when Janet looked up and saw a woman on the narrow path, some distance in front of them.

"Ian, why don't you see if she speaks English. Maybe she can tell us if we're on the right track?"

"Yeah, all right. When we get closer I'll ask her."

As they got nearer to her, however, they realised she was stopping every now and then, looking through the bits of garbage along the trail. She wore a coat, much too warm for the day. Her hair hung down in strands. She scurried along between lumps of detritus, eyes looking only at her business, never up or outward. Soon they were within hailing distance but just as Ian was about to speak the woman ducked off the path so that there was space between her and them. She never looked directly at them, had barely flicked her eyes. It was as though she scented them on the wind.

She carried a plastic bag, bulky with her found things, her scraps of salvage. Her coat was dirty and stained, looking to Janet as though it was virus-ridden. She wore both a grey and ragged skirt and old jogging pants, the elastic missing out of one ankle, so that it flapped like a broken wing above the top of laceless, too-large running shoes. She did not look Spanish, her hair dirty blonde and her skin pale, too pale for this sunny climate.

Ian called out, "Por favor,..." and stepped off the track toward her. She jumped back as if he had thrown a stone and scrambled further away, maintaining her safety zone like a wild dog.

"Ian, you're scaring her! Let me try." Janet tried to look non-threatening, woman to woman, smiled and softly spoke, "Excuse me. Tourists, we're tourists,..." The woman ignored her, moving quickly now, her head down. She stumbled on the uneven, jagged rocks. She turned to Janet and for a moment their eyes met.

In that instant Janet was swamped by a wave of fear, not of the woman, but *from* the woman. She was a wild animal, her mind full of only the instinct thoughts of a coyote or fox. What was this thought? The fear-thought of a wild thing. It poured from her. The cringing need to be apart. The woman was in a place where those of her kind were not of her kind, where they were other and dangerous. Janet wanted to reach the woman, to get through. She felt crippled by a terrible, howling sadness. She longed to be someone who reminded this creature, she belonged, that she was human; to bring her back from the edge with a gesture, some gesture of kindness.

Janet couldn't lose her, couldn't abandon her to her anguish. No one could survive and be that alone. No one could withstand the weight and terror. Not this woman, and not Jackie. She felt panic rise up in her throat like sour bile. Janet couldn't let it happen again. She dove into her purse and came up with a handful of *pesetas*.

"Wait,..." she called as she followed her. The woman would not stop. Janet had the urge to throw the money toward her, but was sure it would only frighten her more. What horrible past would have caused this madness, would have driven a woman, not old, no older than Janet, away into the barren places?

"Janet, I think you'd better just leave her alone."

Waves of emotion passed into Janet and she couldn't stop them. A loneliness so profound, so unblemished, she believed that yes, it would be possible to have all connections wiped out. Loneliness so complete it would be possible, after feeling it, to be able to breathe only in the abandoned places in the world, comfortable only in the company of ghosts. Loneliness so penetrating that any human contact thereafter would be like a mocking brand seared into the skin. Janet gasped and started to cry. *Jackie... Jackie...* The name flew around inside her head like an empty plastic bag caught in a storm gust.

The woman walked away, quickly, but careful not to fall and be injured on the jagged rocks, for who would help a thing such as herself, if she were wounded? Janet kept following, her hand out, the money proffered as though she were the beggar.

"Janet, what the hell are you doing? She doesn't want it. Leave her alone."

"Ian, please, you try! We can't leave her like this! It's terrible!"

Ian stared at her, puzzled, but seeing how upset she was. "I know it's awful, she's probably a drug addict or something, but what can you do about it?"

"No, no, not drugs, that's not it..." But she was unable to describe what it was. Janet jogged a few steps further, and they were almost back out to the construction area now. The woman had moved up the street and opened the lid of a huge garbage bin left near a building site.

"Please Ian..."

"Oh, all right." He took the money and headed toward the woman, but she sensed him coming behind her and whirled around, eyes on him, and she must have seen the money too, but it held no meaning for her. She scuttled behind the bin and moved out across the building site, disappearing around a corner, her eyes glancing back now and then to make sure she wasn't followed.

Janet kept staring at Ian and at the place where the woman had gone. She felt cold, even in the brazen sunlight. She felt as though there was a hole in her chest where a bleak and barren wind blew.

A truck came up the road, carrying three men. They must have seen Ian following the ragged woman. They slowed the truck, stared hard at him as they passed, but moved on. The noise of the truck made Ian turn. He shook his head as though to clear it. He looked across the road at Janet, saw she was crying. He came back to her, stuffing the bills in his pocket, along with the map. He put his arms around her. She was shaking.

"Babe, I'm sorry, but you tried to help. She just doesn't want help, you know. Sometimes there's just nothing you can do. Are you OK?"

Janet burrowed as far into his chest as she could, not caring how they looked, how vulnerable and foolish, two tourists in sensible shoes standing in the middle of a road, far from the tourist attractions.

"I don't want to go to the caves anymore." She felt like a child needing to be comforted.

"No, that's all right. How about we try and catch a cab

Lauren B. Davis

back to the hotel and I'll buy you a bottle of wine with lunch?"

"Can't we tell somebody?"

"Tell them what? Tell who? It's not like she's a stray dog and the SPCA will come and rescue her."

"No, it isn't like that, is it?" Janet clung to him tightly, breathing in his familiar smell, letting his arms around her show her she was not the one abandoned in the barren rocky places of the world. She couldn't get the feelings out of her, couldn't let go of them. She started to sob again, sensing the tatter-faced woman near them somewhere, sniffing through cast off bits of sandwich, competing with rats and roaches for a morsel of something sweet. She could taste mould on her tongue.

Ian held her at arm's length and looked at her smudged face, the lips loose with trembling, the eyes haunted. "No matter where we go in the world... what we see... some things we can't fix... some maybe we can..."

"Did you really understand what she was like? Did you?"

"I don't know," he hesitated, "but it's upsetting anytime you see someone crazy gone like that. And we're in a foreign country, things hit you harder when you're outside what you're used to."

"It's horrible." She clutched her way back inside the safety of his embrace.

"Janet, listen to me," Ian stroked the back of her hair, "I will never let you get lost, do you understand? I would never let you come..." he looked for the word, "unanchored... that way. Do you know that? You need to know that."

Ian felt his wife's fingers relax their grip, ever so slightly.

They went back to the hotel. They lay on the bed of heavy cotton ticking and Janet fell asleep in Ian's arms. He kept his arms around her long after his muscles cramped, and filled his head with the mint-fresh smell of her hair.

Later, when his mother back in Portland asked Ian how Janet had liked Spain, he told her he thought it had done her a world of good, getting away. She'd been able to cut back on her medication, almost in half, which was wonderful. She'd even been able to talk about Jackie's death a little without breaking down completely. He was hopeful, very hopeful.

His mother said how awful it must be to lose a sister, let alone a twin. How she couldn't imagine what it must feel like.

"It feels very lonely, I think." said Ian. "Very lonely."

Lauren B. Davis

In The Memory House

Becky's mother played solitaire on the coffee table, a Matinee cigarette dangling delicately from her lower lip. Now and then she took a sip from her glass of scotch and ginger ale. She wore black Mary Tyler Moore capri pants and the pale yellow sweater with the buttons made out of red plastic cherries. It was a favourite of Becky's father.

Becky, who was six years and five months old, watched *Chez Hélène* on the TV and tried to learn French.

Becky listened very carefully, and repeated "bonjour" and "crayon." She knew she could remember that that meant pencil. She wanted to be able to speak French by the time her father came home, because her mother had told her he was in Paris on business and that Paris was in another country called France and that was where they spoke French all the time. She wondered how she would put the word pencil into a sentence for her father.

She heard his key in the door and jumped up.

"Hey! Bon-ger! Where are my girls?" he called out as he threw open the front door, bringing with him a blast of wet and icy Canadian wind. It picked

Lauren B. Davis

up the solitaire cards and tossed them.

"Daddy! Daddy! Not Bon-ger! Bonjour! You said it wrong. Say Bonjour!" Becky said as he dropped his bags and scooped her up into his arms, up so high she that could touch the light fixture on the ceiling if she wanted to. But now she didn't want to. She just wanted to put her hands on his face, on either side of his big face and feel the bristly roughness of his skin.

"Hi there, Miss Smartie Pants, you been a good girl?"

"Yes I have, I have, you can ask Mommy."

He put her down and she hugged his leg while he greeted his wife.

"I missed you," he said and hugged her.

"Good trip?" She offered only her cheek for kissing.

"Busy. Very busy."

"Must have been."

"I tried to get a minute to call, but you wouldn't believe the way these Frenchies go on. Yack, yack, yack. Meetings all day, all night. Barely had a minute to grab a shower and a couple of hours' sleep. Damn near killed me! But it paid off. We got the deal, even if I didn't have a minute to myself."

She took his coat as he shrugged it off and went to the closet to hang it up. "I worry, you know, when I don't hear from you at all. I even thought of calling the hotel one night."

"Really? Well, you probably wouldn't have found me there. We were in meetings 'til all hours, one night 'til nearly four a.m., would you believe it?"

"Daddy, what did you bring us? Were you too busy for presents?"

"I was awfully busy…"

"But not too busy?"

"Well…"

"Oh, Daddy!"

"I might just have a thing or two."

Becky clapped her hands and ran to the bags he'd dropped by the door.

"Where is it?"

"Hold on a minute Becky, for heaven's sake," her mother

60

said. "Go sit on the couch and give your father a minute to catch his breath before you start grabbing for things."

Becky ran to the couch and bounced down. She knew her mother was excited too. Her father always came back from trips with presents, chocolate and stuffed animals and once a bathing cap with a big flower on the top. She loved that bathing cap so much that even though it was mid-winter, Becky wore it the next day right along with her snowsuit and mittens.

Her father started pulling stuff out of his suitcase, rumpled shirts and socks and underwear.

"Now, I know it's in here somewhere."

"You're just like Marco Polo," her mother said.

"Who's that?" Becky asked.

"A great explorer who spent far too much time away from home, but tried to make everything better when he returned by bribing his family with presents."

"Phyllis!" her father said, clutching his cheeks in mock horror. "Could it be you don't want any presents?"

"I didn't say that."

"That's good, because none of my other girlfriends like this colour." He winked at Becky and passed a package wrapped in pale blue tissue paper to Becky's mother. She opened it and shrieked.

"Oh, Frank, it's absolutely beautiful." She wrapped the silk scarf around her shoulders and ran her fingers over the material. It was white with little blue Eiffel towers scattered all over it and the word "Paris" written in what looked like gold braid around the outside to form a border.

"That's real silk you know, all the way from gay Paree!"

"It's just lovely!" She leaned over the table and gave Frank, who was sitting on the floor, a big kiss.

"But Madame, there's more!" he cried and produced another present from the magic bag. "Perfume for my lady."

"This is really too much," said her mother, although she plucked it from his hand in a flash. Inside was a small bottle, a most mystical deep blue colour with a silver stopper. "Evening in Paris! Oh, I've always wanted Evening in Paris! I love it. I love *you!*"

Lauren B. Davis

"Enough to get us a drink?"

"Oh, I suppose so. But just one, I've got to finish dinner."

As she walked past him he reached out and slapped her behind, causing her to squeal and laugh as she hopped off into the kitchen, one hand rubbing the sore spot.

"What about me?" Becky pleaded, hands clasped under her chin and shoulders hunched with anticipation.

"Let's wait 'til your mother comes back in."

"Mom! Hurry up! Hurry!"

"Oh, good grief, Becky! OK, OK, I'm here." Phyllis came back into the room, holding two full glasses. "Here, baby." She handed one to Frank, who took three big gulps and nearly emptied it.

"Ah!" He smacked his lips and put the glass down. "Now, what could there be in here for Becky? Did I forget it? Gee whiz, maybe I forgot it on the plane." He reached deep into his bag, almost up to his shoulder.

"Oh no, oh Daddy, no!" Becky's heart fell to her knees and her stomach flipped.

"No, it's all right, here it is!" Her father held out an oblong package. She reached for it. "Careful, now careful. That's very delicate."

"Put it down on the table, sweetie," said her mother.

"OK, OK,..." Becky's pudgy little fingers went to work ripping the pink paper. It was heavy. She peeled back the final layer and then opened the lid of the box underneath. "Ooooohhhhh..." she breathed. It was too lovely. Too wonderful.

"Let me help you," her mother said, pulling the heavy object up out of the box and placing it on the table. "Oh, Frank, where did you find this?"

It was a thing more precious, more magical, more perfect, than anything Becky had ever seen. It was a champagne bottle, and in the bottle was champagne, of course, and Becky knew what that was because she'd seen her parents drink it on their wedding anniversary. Floating in the champagne were flecks of gold, tumbling and swirling just like the snow in the little water-filled dome with the snowman inside that her grandmother gave

62

her last year. But that this was so much better! Because in the bottom was a tiny porcelain dancing girl, wearing a white foamy tutu and standing on tiny gold ballet slippers, way up on her toes.

"Here, give it to me, let me show you," said her father. He picked it up and turned it over. Becky could see a small knob on the bottom, which her father turned. Then he set it down again on the coffee table and as he did, strains of the most beautiful music ever heard by anyone began to play. At the same time the little woman in the golden rain began to turn round and round and round, dancing in the fairy kingdom inside the bottle. Becky was afraid she might cry it was so pretty.

"What do you say, Becky?" prodded her mother.

"Oh, Daddy, thank you, thank you, thank you! It's the best thing I've ever had. The best thing I've ever seen. It's my favourite thing forever, I promise." Becky jumped up and ran around the table, careful not to knock it and jar the music box, and threw her arms around his neck, smothering him with kisses, all over his eyes and nose and cheeks and chin and not even minding the smell of the whiskey.

He hugged her back and grinned and laughed and her mother laughed and they were all very happy.

"More drinks, I say! More drinks! I think this calls for a celebration!" Frank said, and Phyllis smiled and went to get the whiskey bottle.

All through dinner Becky kept running back to take a peek at the dancer in the bottle. She discovered a little switch on the side that turned the music on and off, once it was wound up, which was good, because it meant she didn't have to keep turning the bottle over. It was very heavy and she was afraid she'd drop it. She could have spent the rest of her life gazing at that bottle.

When she went to bed her mother made her leave the music box in the living room because she said she didn't want Becky staying up all night playing with it. After all, she had school the next day. She fell asleep with her stuffed bunny under one arm and dreamt dreams of gold-starred skies and toe shoes.

In the morning, first thing, before her mother had even come

Lauren B. Davis

in to wake her, Becky, wearing her footed, flap-door jammies, rushed into the living room. Bunny trailed ear-held along the floor. She couldn't wait to introduce Bunny to the dancing lady.

The coffee table was music box-bare. Her mother must have put it away somewhere. Becky went into the kitchen and found her sitting at the chrome table in her old stained housecoat, drinking coffee and smoking a cigarette.

"Where's my dancer?" she said.

"Don't you even say good morning?"

"Good morning," she was impatient. "Mummy, where'd you put it?"

"Put what?"

"Mummy, don't tease." Teasing wasn't fair. Not about something this important. "Where's Daddy's present?"

"You broke it," she said.

"Broke it?" She pulled Bunny up to her stomach and hugged him.

"Yes."

"No, I didn't. I didn't." Becky's heart was pounding. "Where is it?!"

"Don't you remember? You knocked it off the coffee table last night."

Her mother flicked the ash off the end of her cigarette and looked into her coffee cup for a moment. Then she looked up, directly at Becky, and said it again.

"You broke it."

She looked at her mother. Becky's eyebrows pulled down over her nose. What was happening? Her chin began to tremble. She felt a burning in her chest, under the blue kitty appliqué on her jammies. Her hands formed very small fists. She opened her mouth. Then she closed it. A huge lump moved in her throat. She opened her mouth again.

"That's a lie, that's a lie, a lie!" she screamed over and over.

Her mother said nothing.

Becky fell into a great rushing cyclone of sound, wailing tears and a terrible deep tearing. Her head shook and her arms and legs and hands and feet, flying off in all directions, as though she was being blown up, blown apart. She couldn't stop shrieking at her dry-eyed, coffee-sipping mother.

Later, when she was allowed to come out of her room, where she had had to stay if she was going to act that way, if she was going to work herself up into such a state she couldn't even go to school, she found the thing. Trash can-buried. Even the dancer smashed. Next to the empty whiskey bottles. She felt the muscles in her neck go tight, her eyes began to burn again. She found it very hard to breathe.

She ran a finger along the delicate porcelain leg and the teeny foot in the gold shoe, still attached to the base.

She put the lid back down. She left it there.

They lived in the house with the blue roof then. That's how they always talked about it, as though the roof being blue conferred some sort of spiritual sky-kissed status to the shabby little bungalow. *The Blue Roof, they'd say, that happened when we lived in The Blue Roof.* The story of the music box, however, was never told again.

Lauren B. Davis

Scarecrow

Ivy sleeps, a bird-light bundle curled up in a nest of old flannel nightgown and thick socks, tangled sheets, an Indian blanket and plaid comforter. The top of her head barely shows, just a feathering of short brown curls on the pillow. With tomorrow's first light, she'll be picking her way through the pre-dawn streets to the restaurant. She's expected to be behind the counter and smiling with a fresh pot of coffee by 7:00; ready for the welders and the carpenters, the truckers and the carpet factory shift changers.

At the tentative thump of the first footfall on the stairs her eyes open and she's listening. To awaken instantly alert to every little noise is a blessing and a curse that's been with her since she was a child. The stairs leading up to her door from the alley are metal and the steps sound hollow and heavy. She can't imagine who would be showing up at this hour of night. She looks over at the old wind-up brass clock on the bedside table. It reads 11:15 p.m. The footsteps stop. Her lips purse slightly. Whoever it is knocks. She has half a mind to ignore it; maybe they'll go away. They knock again.

"Ivy, you home?"

Ivy frowns and cocks her head, listening hard. She is not prepared to trust her ears.

"Ivy, it's me, it's Bobbie. You in there?"

Bobbie! Ivy jumps out of bed.

"I'm coming. Wait," she calls out to him. She grabs her quilted robe, folded over the wrought iron foot-board, and hurries through the tiny but immaculate living room. She steps in a sheet of cold light lying on the floor, tossed there by the street lamp outside the window, which faces the main street, and she shivers as though the temperature had actually dropped. She hesitates at the door and ties her robe tighter about her waist. She turns the deadbolt and opens the door. In front of her stands her brother, Bobbie.

The last time Ivy saw her brother he was fifteen. Now he is nearly twenty. He stands in the harsh glare from the security light in the back parking lot. The stark grey tinge does nothing to improve his skin tone. He's wearing army fatigue pants, the kind with pockets on the side of the legs. He wears heavy black lace-up boots and a jacket that's intended to be leather, but falls far short of fooling anyone. His dark blonde hair is long and none too clean. He's taller than he was when Ivy last saw him. He must be nearly six feet, taller by six inches than Ivy. He hasn't put any meat on his bones though, and looks like an undernourished surplus store scarecrow, with his pants flapping around his skinny thighs in the cold wind. At his feet sits a duffel bag.

He looks like he just got out of the detention centre, though Ivy knows he left McGregor Hall when he was sixteen. Went to a halfway house until he turned eighteen, which is when she lost track of him.

Bobbie looks behind him, ducking his head around the side of the building to look down the alley, out onto Prince Street and back again. He bounces on his toes and cups his bare red hands around his mouth, blowing to warm them. On his right hand is a tattoo spelling "Honour", on the left "Loyalty".

"Hey, ain't you even going to let me in? I'm freezing my ass out here." When he grins at her, Ivy sees he's missing a tooth on the left side.

"Yeah,… of course, come in, quick… "

Ivy closes the door as he steps over the threshold and turns toward him. He puts his duffel bag down and for a moment they stand looking at each other, then he moves to give her a hug, but it's awkward, like hugging a stranger, all shaky and sharp. After a second they fall away.

"So, how you been, Sis?"

"Fine, OK. How did you know where I was? Did you go by the house? Did you see Dad?"

"Steve Thompson told me where you were living. I bumped into him in Halifax, eh? 'Bout eight months ago. He told me you were living over the laundry mat, working at the Schooner."

"I can't believe you're here. Where the hell have you been for the past two years? We didn't know what happened to you. Dad tried to find out, but they said you were eighteen and legal and if you didn't want us to know where you were, there was nothing we could do. "

"Yeah, like Dad suddenly gives a shit." Ivy decides to let this pass. "I just had to get lost, you know? I had stuff going on." He does not elaborate. "So, listen, how about something to eat?" Bobbie starts over to the kitchen alcove. "You got any booze?" He takes off his jacket and tosses it on the couch.

"No, I don't. I can probably make some scrambled eggs. You want a coffee?"

"Yeah, I guess."

"OK, sit down. I'll get it." Bobbie moves back into the living room area, starts pacing around, looking at the dance prints on the wall, the books on the brick and plank shelves. He turns the radio on, then turns it off again. He's making her nervous, won't settle anywhere. Now and then he goes to the window, moves the curtain aside and looks at the dark street below. She wonders whether he's high on something.

Ivy goes to the refrigerator and finds eggs, milk and butter, a little cheddar cheese. There's not much else in there. A carton of orange juice, some baloney slices curled up and dried out around the edges, a couple of tomatoes and some bacon. She takes a bowl from the cupboard, a whisk from the drawer. She cracks

Lauren B. Davis

the eggs, adds milk, salt and pepper. She glances over her shoulder to see what Bobbie's doing. He's back at the front window, fiddling with the curtains.

"Bobbie, land someplace, OK?"

Bobbie closes the curtains but remains where he is, looking out from the crack where the panels join, onto Prince Street. Ivy concentrates on the frying pan, the creamy mixture of eggs and milk. She is unsettled by the hour, by the strangeness of her brother here after so long.

"So, what are you doing in town? You back to stay?"

"Nah, I'm just here for a couple of days maybe. I might even leave tomorrow, we'll see." He crosses to the table and sits down, watching Ivy cook. He taps on the tabletop, making drumsticks of his fingertips.

"You got a job?"

"I had one, eh? Had a couple of jobs. When I got out of the halfway house I was at the Jukebox, this record store, but I was only there for a few months. They were assholes. I worked at other stuff though, manual stuff, and in a restaurant for a while. I hated that though, clearing up after people I shouldn't have to clean up after, you know what I mean? White trash and niggers."

Ivy opens her mouth to say something, to tell him not to use that word, but she's so shocked she doesn't react quickly.

"Anyway, I ain't got a job right now."

"So where are you living?" she asks. Maybe it's best to let it pass, for now. She hasn't seen him in so long. She doesn't want to start off with an argument. When did he start talking like that? It tripped off his tongue so easily…

"I'm just hanging out at friends' places. But not for long. I had a place with Bill and Gary, these two guys from the centre. They're great guys. They taught me a lot of stuff about what's really going on in the world."

"Why," she grinned at the thought of Bobbie sitting around late at night talking politics and philosophy, "what's really going on in the world?"

"You probably wouldn't understand."

"Try me."

"About the new order coming. We have to protect ourselves, you know. White people."

"I never think of white people as needing much protection."

"You've been brainwashed by the Zionists."

"What on earth are you talking about? Zionists?" She laughs, hoping he'll join in. "You're not becoming a conspiracy theory freak, are you, little brother?"

"I said you wouldn't understand."

She doesn't know what to say. She remembers a day about a year after their mother disappeared. She was just a kid, maybe ten or eleven, and they'd been to the junky little carnival set up in the parking lot of the A&P grocery store. She was using a handkerchief dampened with her own spit to wipe away the sticky aftermath of cotton candy from Bobbie's mouth. She wishes she could just as easily wipe away the words he's now speaking.

"Are you still living with these guys?"

"Naw. We couldn't keep up the rent after I lost my job and this Jew landlord wouldn't give us a break. So I'm just staying with different friends right now. It's OK though. I got really great friends."

"*Jew* landlord?"

"Yeah, shit, the guy was an asshole. You know what they're like."

Ivy looks at him over the frying pan, her eyebrow raised. He stares back at her. This is not the boy she knew. Ivy has no idea how he has become what he is, and the mystery of that is as frightening as the knowledge that she is powerless to undo it. She can no more deconstruct who he is now than she can un-ring a bell.

She takes a plain white china plate from the cupboard and puts the eggs on it. She puts instant coffee granules in two matching blue cups and pours in the boiling water

"What do you take? Milk?" She realises she doesn't know him anymore.

"Yeah, and sugar." Ivy prepares the coffee, gets a fork and knife and brings the food to the table, puts it in front of Bobbie, straightening the cutlery on either side of the plate as she does so.

"Just like at work, eh?" Bobbie grins again, and again Ivy notices the missing tooth.

"How'd you lose the tooth?"

He brings his hand up to his mouth, as though he were trying to hide the gap.

"Ah, shit, got into a fight back in the centre. Some bullshit thing. No big deal. But I messed the guy up. He didn't fuck with me again."

Ivy doubts this, but doesn't let on. "Was it bad in there?"

"Not so bad. I met some guys, made some friends."

"You know I would have come to see you more, but you said you didn't want me to."

"I know. What was the point?"

"The point is, you're my brother. I love you." Ivy reaches over and takes his hand, the one with "Loyalty" tattooed on it. He pulls away, leans back in his chair.

"I wrote you, you never wrote back, " she says.

"Not much to say. How about: 'Having a wonderful time, wish you were here?'" Bobbie leans into his food again, finishing off the eggs in a few bites. "You sure you don't got any beer?"

"Positive. Sorry."

"No big deal."

They sit in silence for a few minutes, drink their coffee. Bobbie taps his fingers on the table.

"You going to go see Dad? He'd love to see you. We could go over there tomorrow, after I get off shift."

"I don't want to see him. I'm probably going to leave tomorrow anyway."

"You should see him..."

"Fuck that! The second he slapped me across the face in that courtroom was the second he stopped being my old man. I didn't even think he'd show up. Wish he hadn't."

"Bobbie, he was mad. You can't really blame him, you stole a goddamn car, had a drunken crash, put Chris McDonald in a wheelchair..."

"It was Chris' idea!"

"Maybe, but you were driving!"

Bobbie stands up, nearly knocking the chair over as he does.

He walks back to the window, looks out through the curtains again. He remains with his back to Ivy, the wings of his shoulder blades held up high and pinched together, clearly visible through the thin fabric of his blue check shirt. Chicken wings. He must be freezing out there if that's all he has to wear, Ivy thinks. He still looks like such a kid.

"Look, I'm sorry, OK?" Ivy comes over to him, stands beside him. "I didn't mean to upset you. It's all in the past now anyway."

"Yeah, well." He runs his palm around the back of his neck, tilting his head to the side, as though his neck was sore, trying to work a crick out. As he does so, Ivy can see another tattoo on his neck, naively done, home-made. It looks like a swastika, but she can't be sure.

She comes around in front of him and perches on the side of the windowsill. Her stomach feels a little queasy from the coffee and she's suddenly very tired. She wants to be curled up beneath the covers of her warm quiet bed.

"You know Bobbie, I'm really glad to see you, but it's late and I've got to be up early. We can catch up more tomorrow. You want to crash on the couch?"

"I guess... listen, Ivy..."

"Yeah?"

"It's just that, I'm kinda in a jam, you know..."

"What kind of jam?"

"I just need some money, not much, five hundred maybe..."

"What's going on, Bobbie?" Ivy is now awake, her fingertips tingling.

"Nothing. I just need some cash, OK? Is that so much to ask?"

"I don't have five hundred just like that, lying around..."

"Shit, Ivy, you have the money, you can spare a little, come on!"

"Bobbie, I do not have that kind of money. Read my lips!"

Bobbie turns and looks around the room for a minute, his eyes scanning the couch, the chair, the television set, the shelves of books. Then he seems to find what he's looking for, walks quickly across the room and picks up Ivy's brown leather purse that has been sitting on a table near the front door.

"Bobbie, put that down!" Ivy dashes across the room and tries to grab the purse from him. For a moment they are in a tug of war, then Bobbie reaches in, grabs her wallet and lets the strap of the purse go. Ivy stumbles backward and collides with the arm of the couch. Bobbie rifles through the wallet, but finds only thirty dollars. He throws the wallet on the floor in disgust.

"Don't you have any more? Where do you hide it? You must have some more!"

Ivy's heart is lurching against the bars of her birdcage ribs. What is happening here? This red-eyed rat-bag boy in front of her is a stranger. She wants him not to be here. She wants to go back to bed. The room is too small for them both; there is not enough air to breathe. Whatever is happening here, she wants it to be over.

"You want to wait until Monday, I can get some more out of the bank. I've got a couple of hundred in the bank."

Bobbie strides over to her, his limbs stiff with anger, then sits down heavily on the couch, as though the joints in his legs have given out. He puts his elbows on his bony knees and rests his head in his hands.

"I can't wait that long. I gotta go. Now."

"What the hell is going on?" Ivy has her hand in front of her mouth as she speaks, as though trying to hush herself, advising herself to ask no questions. "What have you done, Bobbie?"

"I got into something, OK? It had to be done. She needed to be taught a lesson. She's a race traitor. Fucking bitch."

"Who are you talking about? What is this 'race traitor' shit?" Ivy's forehead is starting to hurt, the words are reaching her ears, but she can't understand them. There is a noise, like a mass of dark-winged crows, flapping up a whirlwind, a dust devil.

"It's not shit! I learned a lot in the past few years. Lots of things. About the race war coming, about how soon there won't be any white people left, the way the niggers are breeding. We have to protect our race against the mud races. This girl, see,

Nancy, she's a traitor to her race. She was going out with this nigger. She used to go with Gary and then she left him and went with this *nigger*! It's a sexual deviation, white women who like to sleep with blacks. They get into some kind of weird sex trip, it's like bestiality or something like that. It's disgusting!"

Ivy feels sick to her stomach now, the coffee churning around like black greasy water in her belly. Bobbie's voice comes from a long way off, spinning out venom, spitting out poison. The room feels like a hollow drum and the word, that foul word, bangs against the taut skin over and over again. If he would just be quiet for a minute, let her think...

"We warned her. We warned her to stay with her own kind. Stay away from that nigger. You have to be strong, man, have to be able to defend your own. She just wouldn't listen to reason, you know? We had to scare her, had to teach her, that's all we wanted to do..."

"Bobbie, I don't want..."

"Don't want what, Sis? Listen, it's her fault, she's the traitor, the pervert! If she'd listened to reason... we had to make an example. Halifax is a sewer for race mixers. The three of us, we followed her and that coon, got them near the park. Guy was an asshole, man, started all this martial art shit, we had to fight back. Nigger punch me, I'm going to try to *kill* his ass. It's a battle, man! She got in the way. She got in the way."

"Did you kill her?" Ivy grabs him by the shoulders and shakes him. "Did you!"

"I think so. I don't know, I think so. I had an axe handle. She went down. There was a lot of blood." He is shaking now, hugging himself.

"You didn't wait and see? Did you try to help her? What about the man?"

"Who cares about the nigger!?!"

"Stop it! Stop using that word! Tell me!"

"The guy was bleeding you know, but I think it was just a couple of broken bones, maybe some ribs, his nose, I don't know! I wasn't going to hang around and wait until his buddies showed up! I took off. It's her own fault."

Lauren B. Davis

"You can't run."

"You think I'm going to walk up to some black cop, some Jew lawyer and ask for help? I got to go! *You* got to help me."

"What's happened to you? You're crazy. You have to stop, just stop. You have to turn yourself in."

"Now you're the one who's crazy. You get me the money and I'm going to head down to the States, where the Aryan Nation headquarters are, I'm going to hide out. I'm going to be a fucking hero with these guys!"

Ivy backs away from him. She hugs her bathrobe to her chest. She stands with her feet apart, as though on the deck of a rolling ship. She needs to keep her balance. She doesn't want him to run. She wants him to look at the woman, lying on the pavement, the man lying next to her. She wants him to stop running, to turn and face the choices he has made, the actions he has taken, to see as lies those things he has adopted as truth. She takes a deep breath and squares her shoulders.

"I'm not giving you any money, Bobbie. I'm not going to help you run. I'll go to the police with you and I'll stand beside you every step of the way, but you can't run from this. You'll be running forever."

"Please, come on!" His voice is shrill, high-pitched and his face red.

"No."

"Fuck you!"

"Fine. Fuck me."

Bobbie's face looks full of sharp places, his cheekbones brittle under the skin, a scar under his eye in the shape of a small star. What could have made a scar like that? When did it happen? Sometime when she wasn't looking, when she wasn't there. His eyebrows are startling; they are so dark against the white pasty skin, the dark blonde hair. Their father's eyebrows. But on Dad they look like a good idea, a surprise in his face. On Bobbie they look like war paint, drawn for effect, and the effect is not kind.

"I don't guess I should expect anything else from you, Sister. Like mother, like daughter. Looks like the blood runs deep. Looks like the blood will out."

76

"What the hell are you talking about now?"

"You never did get it, did you? How could you be so stupid, so blind all these years? Sitting in the house, playing little mama, doing the laundry, the cooking. Never having any friends, too good for everybody else. Well, everybody else knew. Why do you think nobody ever came to our house after *she* left? Why do you think we were always the odd family? Everybody knew except you! Why do you think she left? Who do you think she left with!?!"

"We never knew where she went. Nobody knew..." There is a glass cat scratching at the inside of Ivy's skin, right under her heart.

"She left with Fred Warren, that *nigger* from Cherrybrook!" He made an ugly snorting sound. "Not that she stayed with him. And he even had the nerve to show up at Dad's job, blubbering like a baboon, to see if she'd come back here after she ran off on him! And Dad fucking tried to console him! In front of all the guys on the loading dock! It was the town joke! Dad a two-time fool! Don't you get it, Ivy? You never thought about it? How Mum and Dad were supposed to have met in Halifax, she got pregnant and then they married and came back here? Christ, she was seven months pregnant when they came here, Aunt Ella told me! Dad had only been in Halifax for three weeks!" He's shrieking and spitting on her, right up in her face. She can smell the coffee on his breath, the eggs and cheese.

"If somebody'd taught *her* a lesson we'd all be better off. Go look in the mirror, Ivy. Little tanned? Hair kinda kinky? Figure it out. You know what they say, once they get a taste for it..." He pauses and starts to laugh, which is odd, because he's also crying and angrily wiping the tears away with the back of his hand, the one with the word "Honour" tattooed on it. "You stupid bitch! You..."

"Bobbie, stop this now..."

"You...NIGGER!"

Ivy doesn't think she saw it coming. One minute she's standing on the carpet near the couch and the next she's on the floor. Simple as that. One minute she's up and the next she's down.

Lauren B. Davis

Her first thought is that it should hurt more, but it doesn't really. Her upper lip feels as though she's been at the dentist, numb and a little tingly, nothing more.

Ivy stays where she is. There doesn't seem to be any reason to get up. Bobbie is making himself at home, scattering books from the brick and plank shelves, opening cupboards and rummaging through drawers, throwing onto the floor anything he doesn't deem useful. He moves into the bedroom. She hears him slamming things around. Ivy doesn't want her rooms destroyed. She wants her belongings to remain intact.

"There's fifty dollars in the music box on the top of the dresser," she calls. "Take it."

He comes back into the living room, the fragile box in his hands. He pockets the bills without bothering to count them, tosses the box on the coffee table where it comes to a rattling stop. A few tinkly notes from "The Anniversary Waltz" chime weakly. Bobbie picks up his jacket and shrugs into it. He picks up his duffel bag and opens the door. Before he leaves he turns and blows her a kiss.

"Sure has been nice seeing you again, Sis. Give my love to dear old Dad." Bobbie slips down the stairs, leaving the door open behind him. His boots tromp a hollow chorus down the metal steps into the alley. An icy tendril slinks into the room. Ivy stares at the spot where he had been. Her mind refuses to work at the same speed at which the rest of the world seems to be moving. It's as though she's experiencing everything a few minutes after it actually happens. A self-protecting time delay. A ghost-shiver passes through her. She picks herself up, walks across the chill wooden floor and closes the door. She locks it, throws the deadbolt and slides the chain in the hook. She crosses the room and opens the curtains.

Bobbie walks quickly down the deserted street, past Ethel's Gift Shop and Rossy's Five and Dime, past The Blue Schooner Restaurant where Ivy is expected to be in just a few hours. He keeps to the pools of shadows just outside the range of the street lamps. She can see his breath coming in foggy bursts around his head, crystallising in the arctic air. He moves like a ragged mouse caught outside his hole.

She leans her forehead against the glass, melting the thin layer of ice formed around the frame of the window. She strains to see Bobbie for a second longer as he rounds the corner and then he's gone, a sharp and jagged shadow. She does not want to move her head from the cold surface; the pain it brings is cleansing somehow. But she unwillingly accepts she must move, must think, must attempt to make some sense of it all.

Ivy slides down the wall and sits on the floor. She is crying. There is no noise accompanying this crying, the tears are simply sliding, one after the other, down her face, to drip into the top of her housecoat.

Are the things Bobbie said true? She must think about that. They feel true. Had she known, before tonight, she was not her father's daughter? It's hard to decide. The news does not feel new. It feels as though she already knew. There is no thwack of shock, only a mere bubble of recognition, like the sound a duck makes when it pops up to the surface of a lake after a long time under water.

She heaves herself up and moves to the table. Pushes aside the plate. The leftover bits of egg have congealed into unwholesome rubbery globs. Her stomach lurches. She takes the coffee mug, reheats the water. She needs caffeine. She needs to think clearly. When the coffee is made she sits on the couch and wraps her hands around the heat. She stares into the dark liquid. The small apartment is oddly quiet now. It's an edgy stillness, tinny with anticipation.

She takes a sip, being careful of her swollen lip which now hurts quite a bit. Soon it will be morning and there will be things to do. She will have to see her father. The police probably. She will have to call the restaurant and tell them she won't be in. Things will move quickly, and so this parenthetic moment is to be cherished. She's grateful for these hours, when most of the world she knows is still sleeping, as yet unaware of the terrible things that can happen when you're not looking.

Ivy finds herself in an oddly analytical frame of mind. She supposes it must be shock. She feels as though she's been absent from her whole life. It's all been going on around her and she's been in her own world, like an autistic child.

She stands, pushes back her chair and walks into the bathroom. It is a small and tidy space, all white tiles and blue towels. It smells faintly of pine. Shells are pasted around the mirror over the sink. Her hands rest on the cool enamel and she gazes at her face, trying to see it as a stranger would.

No matter how she looks, turns her head, angles herself, she finds no clues in the mirror.

It is a pretty face, which is just a fact, and doesn't help in determining the answer to her question. Ivy has always known she is pretty and has, to her credit, remained ambivalent about it. *Pretty is as pretty does*, Aunt Ella used to say. She has dark brown hair with a bit of an auburn polish to it, if you see it in the sunlight. She wears it in a cap of short unruly curls, which is the easiest way of handling hair that turns into a mess of tangles if allowed to grow any longer than the bottom of her ears. Beneath brows that are sparser and not as clearly shaped as those of her father or brother, her eyes are a dark green with yellow speckles and are framed with thick lashes. Her cheekbones are high and prominent, her nose straight and rather longer than the pert turned up noses of girls picked to be cheerleaders, which bothers Ivy not at all as she has never had any desire to be a cheerleader. Her skin is smooth and she never looks pale, but she never manages to tan either, just going from her normal skin tone to crispy red in a short hour. Her mouth is small and nicely shaped, except at the moment because one side is swollen.

It doesn't matter.

It matters that she may not be her father's daughter, for she loves her father and has wanted to be the best of him. As to the other issue, well, the person for whom it seems to matter most has already left the building.

Four hours ago she was asleep, dreaming a dream she'd dreamt before. She dreamt of a house, ramshackle and vast, room after room, some inhabited and some abandoned, with entire wings fallen to disrepair and unforgiving weather.

She wonders what her father is dreaming right now. She'll wait a few hours. While he can, let him sleep.

Blue Valentines

This is what we were listening to: we were listening to Tom Waits singing. The song was about a man who'd ruined his life because he'd hurt the only woman he'd ever loved, so badly that she left him and never came back. She haunts him though.

> *She sends me blue Valentines*
> *All the way from Philadelphia...*

Danny was drinking. Danny was always drinking. I think maybe he only told me he loved me when he was drinking. He sat on the brown plaid couch and I sat on the floor in front of him and he tangled his fingers in my hair. I ran my nails along his thighs and felt his muscles jump.

It was snowing outside. I remember that. Snowing so hard the late afternoon light coming in through the window looked bright even though it was almost dark.

I'd never loved anyone the way I loved him and it didn't matter to me that we fought as much as we did. I couldn't get enough of him. His smell was like good strong coffee first thing in the morning. I could bury my head under his arm and never want to come up for air.

I don't know what he was thinking just then. I used to think I understood him, but now I'm not so sure. He led a whole other life away from me; a life full of caramel-and ivory-skinned girls and needles and guys with home-made tattoos. But at the time I didn't know any of that.

What he did took me by surprise. He lifted me up and held me on his lap with my face buried in his shoulder so I couldn't see him. I tried to pull back but he wouldn't let me.

"If I ever fuck up, I mean really fuck up," he said, "you do what it says in the song. Send me blue Valentines, all the way from wherever you are." His hands were like hungry steel around my neck and waist.

We sat like that for a long time, long after the record had finished.

"Promise me," he whispered.

"I promise," I said.

But I never did. Why should I be the one to keep a promise?

The Poet's Corner

A man lies on a ledge in the Church Street Subway. A shaggy tumble of textures and shapes. Nothing bright about him. Grey and dingy and some things that were blue but are now not, some things that were green but are no longer. His hair could be brown or grey or blonde or red but is not so much colour at all now, but texture of brush or snag of thick torn wool or something badly spun from salty hemp. Bottles and bags and a take-out dish that has not held food for weeks but may still hold the enchantment that is the seed of future food - a few coins. The tile underneath him is wet, I think, and my nose wrinkles, expecting. But it is not liquid leaking from body or bottle but is polished by a man writhing towards sleep. Mirror-bright, cleaned by transference to pores and fibres filled with our discarded things, our shed things, our expelled breath.

He turns and shifts the lumpen weight of layers and flesh. A face is revealed, mired behind a carapace of bristles and bleary soot. I hurry on. I do not want to be caught staring at this human car crash.

I feel a draft of memory. There is some resemblance to a boy I knew. This scraggle of limbs cannot be that boy. Can only be someone similar in structure to that boy.

The day presses on. It is made-up of the cosmetics counter behind which I stand, the fragrances and dabs and shades dispensed as medicine to the hypochondriacs of beauty. A lunch of salad in a plastic tray. My feet ache at day's end, my calf muscles knotted, veins foretelling an unhappy dotage. I am a work-weary horse heading home, quicker to stable at evensong than to field and plow at matins. I pay no mind to fellow commuters.

His form draws me like metal to magnet. His back is turned, a hump of sack, tossed to the side of traffic. A dead dog carcass of a man, lice ridden and forgettable. I am gone to bed and tea and quiet.

Morning's tide pushes me up against the breakers of workaday humanity. I suck in fresher air as the subway doors open. I step onto the platform. He sits facing me. I cannot help but glance. I feel the blood rush to my face, invading by recognition the terrible intimacy of his public invisibility. He is a refuse heap of odours and scraps, from which peer unmistakable leaf-green eyes. This cannot be. And yet this man, this remnant, is my coffee partner from the college, thirteen years past. He was a poet. This antiquity is my one-time friend, Roddy Daniels. No, not friend, but I knew him.

My legs are past him now. But he is all I see, in every face on every advertisement: for fast cars, for expensive watches, for Guinness beer and tiny Nokia telephones. I cannot banish his discarnate shred. I am sure the relic is he.

By noon I am sure I was mistaken.

That night I have dinner with friends in a restaurant where Monet's lilac-filled gardens are painted on the plates. I eat every morsel of the *fera de lac* in *beurre rouge*, every tiny pearl of onion, each spring wand of asparagus. I dare not leave a parsley sprig.

When I leave for work next morning I place four oranges and a loaf of poppy seed bread in my tapestry bag. I sit on the subway with a furrow between my eyes, a skittery rat in my stomach. If he is still there. He has appeared mysteriously. He may well be gone. But if he is there, I will speak to him. Beyond that, my mind makes no commitments.

"Excuse me," I say.

His eyes are watery, the lower lids loose, hanging down slightly, revealing red rims. I hold out the bread. I have not brought a knife. His hands reach out. They are peppered with black. The nails are soot crescents. An infected hangnail festers. He takes the bread. It is Roddy. There is no doubt.

"I brought you these oranges, too."

He begins to peel one, the sticky juice running down his hands leaving trails. I think to offer him a tissue but don't, knowing such a small fragile square could do little to improve the state of him.

"Thank you." His voice is soft and gravelly, deeper than I remember. I think he does not speak much. Up close he has not aged that much. He looks hard ridden and put away wet. There is the stench of the unwashed and the unhealthy about him.

I stand in front of him, the hem of my good Scottish wool coat brushing one of the brown smeared plastic bags that huddle around his feet. I want to pull my coat away, but don't want to offend him. I fear pathogen, bacterium.

"Do you mind if I ask your name?"

"Why do you want to know my name?"

"You don't have to tell me if you don't want."

"I don't have to do anything I don't want to, " he says.

"Of course not," I say.

He looks at me and he does not look angry, but you can never tell. He fills his mouth with fruit, showing mossy teeth.

"I hope you enjoy the oranges." I have made an effort, am exonerated.

"You are June." So, he knows I know him.

"I didn't recognise you at first, Roddy."

"I've changed a bit. Things change."

"So, how are you?" I say, so banal a phrase, but I can find no other.

"I'm fine. How are you?"

"Good. Good." I am silent then. He is noisy with fruit and

Lauren B. Davis

juice and soggy looking teeth and gums. "May I sit down?"

He motions to the plastic seat screwed with a steel rod into the ledge near where he has made his camp. I sit. Smile at him, I hope encouragingly.

"I have to ask. What's happened to you?"

"There isn't much to tell. Why, why do you want to know?"

"It's a shock, seeing you here, this way. I'd like to help." I've said it now, although I had not intended to do so. I realise I am holding my purse so tightly the brass clasp is cutting into my palm. I make an effort to relax. I am further in deep water than I like. I don't know what help means in this context. What would his expectations be? "If you want help, that is..."

"What would you do for me? If I pass your test? Take me home? Feed me? Bathe me? Take me to the vet for shots?"

"I didn't mean to offend you."

"Am I a revolting spectacle?"

"I have to get to work." I stand. I look at my watch, that wellspring of excuses. "Maybe I'll see you again."

I am a coward, but I want to be gone.

"Before you go,..." His hand is out. Of course, he wants some money.

"Yes, certainly, here take this," I scramble in my purse for bills, hand him a ten. His face becomes a bright penny when he smiles, even with those teeth.

"Thank you, June." He laughs and rubs the money between his hands.

I jitter up the stairs to the street. I look back and Roddy raises his hand and waves at me, the bill becomes a handkerchief.

That night I take a taxi home. I take a bus and long walk to work the next day.

I spend the day arranging bottles and jars, dispensing creams and unguents. I flatter saggy skin and sell the dreams of beauty. As the day comes to a close I consider. I could go above ground, take a bus. I could take a taxi. I could avoid the underneath of the city. I walk undecided along the street and then stop at the deli near the subway entrance. I buy a take-out sandwich, ham and cheese, with extra tomatoes and lettuce, and a large coffee. I approach like a penitent.

He eats with gusto. "This is good," he says and smacks his lips.

"Do you get enough to eat?"

"You wouldn't believe what people throw away. There are ways. Places to go where they'll feed you. "

"Ah," I say, as though I understand.

He eats the sandwich in a hurry, nearly finished before I am gone.

This becomes our ritual. Breakfast of bread and fruit, a supper of sandwiches and coffee, always coffee. I know so little about what happens when I'm not there. What does he have in all those bags and why are there four or five some days, eight or nine on others? At times he is "better" than others. Some days he smiles and chatters. Other days he fidgets and scratches and talks of dogs and darkness. It is nearly a week before I dare to ask any more questions.

"Are you all right here, living this way?" We have found a way to speak, although I am still stumbling over words. I have no vocabulary for this.

"This is a good place."

"It seems a hard life. Can I ask... well, what happened?"

"Things fall apart. The centre does not hold. Mere anarchy is loosed upon the world. Yeats was clear. Waves come in and crash down."

"I don't understand."

"Understand? What is there to understand in chaos, the prime mover disappeared in flagrant disregard for promises made? What is there to comprehend when all the hands have fallen off the clocks?" His voice is rising, pitched higher. He attracts attention, his arms wave.

It has been clear from the beginning that he is not, in his mind, what he once was. He had been fragile, always, I remem-

Lauren B. Davis

ber this. I had been drawn to the gentleness of him, but thought him even then unfit for life outside the cloister or the academic cloak. Now I am embarrassed and a little frightened of him.

"It doesn't matter, Roddy. I'll let you finish your food in peace." I stand.

"I haven't come completely undone, if that's what you think," he says, sensing I think him mad. Roddy reaches out his hand, but stops before he touches me. "I am sometimes unclear. But certain things may only be alluded to and not discussed directly. It is an uncertain prospect. Stay,..." I sit back down, and am ashamed to know I wish I'd never started this.

"...went to graduate school after..." Roddy is talking now, "but when I started my thesis I began to have, spells... I got lost a lot. There were dark dogs, slender and deadly. I could see them, outside the dorm. They circled around and around the quad. I didn't go out. Stayed in my room. Didn't eat. Papered over the windows. Plugged my ears against their howling..." He shook his head as though to clear his vision. "Eventually I was picked up by the police, or so I'm told. I was in an intersection, saying some things... I don't remember a lot of that time... I was in hospital for a while... they let me out. Now I'm here."

"I'm really sorry, Roddy. Don't you have any family who could help?"

"No, help is just an empty shelf in a cupboard. My parents are dead. The vivisectionist has become his own subject. I have a sister, Cathy, but she lives somewhere,... somewhere else..."

I reach over and pat Roddy's hand, but he looks past me and doesn't seem to notice.

My sleep that night is vague and elusive. I dream of windswept sand and whirlwinds. I rise at the darkest hour and sit by the window. I look at the urban moonscape, barren and cold. My apartment is small. Two tiny rooms. Space for only me and only then because I do not crave for things. I am content with my minimalist decor, clear of clutter. A white futon, clean surfaces, a vase of mauve tulips, a bowl of polished stones. There is a shelf of books. At thirty-eight I live alone by choice and am drawn to solitary places. There has been clutter in my past, a marriage filled with loud emotions and louder silences. A child that never was. I am more ordered this way. I am satisfied in my ways and myself.

There is no room for anyone else.

I give up on sleep. I drink coffee from a turquoise bowl with no handles. I see Roddy's face in the muddy mirror.

Several days later he recites poetry for me:

"I thought of Dylan Thomas today," he says. "'Within his head revolved a little world\Where wheels, confusing music, confused doubts,\Rolled down all images into the pits\Where half dead vanities were sleeping curled\Like cats, and lust lay half hot in the cold.' It seems to me there was much he understood."

"You used to write poetry. Do you still?" It is a stupid thing to say, as though words would have any purpose, any currency here.

"No, but I remember words. They never disappear. They are in the atoms, in the photons; we are the stuff that stars are made of... stardust memories... Do you have children?" He asks suddenly.

"No. I was married. It didn't work out. There were no children."

"That's too bad. Children are very good to know."

"I suppose they are, if you don't mind the noise. Listen, Roddy, when you were in hospital did they give you medication? Do you still see a doctor?"

"No. Pills and salves and bandages all buffer you. It is a question, sometimes, of geography. Of knowing where you are in relation to the dangers of tooth and claw... Do you still write?"

"No. I never write anything anymore either."

"It's a pity, isn't it, when you look at it this way," he says, and I am unsure as to which way he means.

We grow more comfortable each time we meet. He becomes familiar to me. I look forward to the ritual of seeing him.

"Did you have a good day at work, June?"

"It was a day like any day, busy and crowded with people buying cosmetics they don't need."

"With make-up everyday is Mardi Gras, I would think. Or maybe Halloween. Tell me, do you live alone? Are you in love?"

I am used to his non-sequiters, but I don't want to answer this question. We have been careful of boundaries. "No, I'm not in love. I have a small flat."

"Is it enough for you?"

"Yes. It's enough. I like to live simply."

"You don't get lonely?"

"Doesn't everyone get lonely?"

"I wouldn't know about everyone. Everyone does not concern me. Everyone is a fallacious construct. You sell masks for people. I can understand the attraction in the disguise. There are times the faces are frightening. But generally speaking, I am safer here."

"Safer than where?" I ask.

"Above. "

"You mean on the streets?"

"It can be dangerous outside, above and beyond. You have only to read the news to know of the horrors." Roddy removes a scrap of cloth from the top of one of his many bags and begins to pull out tatters of newspaper, which lay hidden beneath. His hands are full of headlines. They all speak of one atrocity or another. *Woman and child murdered by ex-husband. Video store clerk runs amok, kills four. Man kills girlfriend with crossbow. Homeless man set afire by high school students. Fire kills seven at home for the elderly.* And the rather ludicrous *Carrot-eating woman gives birth to rabbit-eared boy.* "People think they hide these things from me by throwing out the papers, but I rescue the news. There are holes in the sky. I prefer to have something solid above me. I am preparing to move further in." He gazes off down the dark subway tunnel.

"You want to live in the tunnels?" The darkness, the cold, the unknown, seem to creep along the platform. I shiver.

"There are communities beneath the city. Do you not remember your Ellison? The Invisible Man? 'Here, at least, I could try to think things out in peace, or, if not in peace, in quiet. I would take up residence underground. The end was in the beginning.' The mole people have been among us for a very long time. I am gathering myself so that I might be included in their number. It is part of a natural progression."

"But Roddy, how would you...?" I stop here, unable to find a word for what I'm feeling. Survive? No. Survival, at least, is possible in many places, many states of being.

"It is not as you might imagine. There are many who have found the world above to be too lacking in ethics, too violent, too unsuited to the flowering of some plants. A certain network has been devised. There is an order. Chaos is above - below is simple harmony. I believe there may be use for me." He leans toward me, hides his mouth with his hand. "I have been approached."

"By whom?"

"Is it possible to trust you this far? You must vow silence - say it!"

"I'll keep your secrets, Roddy." He watches my face for signs of betrayal, then relaxes, his fingers working their way through his crusty beard over and over again.

"It really doesn't matter," he says. "We are the shadows and can be gone as quickly as the flicker of a candle flame. We are sweet phantoms, elusive as dreams." He chuckles. "It is an honour. I have come to the attention of certain people who have influence below. They are in need of scholars. You may find it hard to believe, but there are children to be taught by teachers who understand what is important. This is the poetry of the religion of humanity. I am hopeful."

I have heard rumours of homeless people who have retreated into the subway tunnels. "I have no right to advise you on what to do, but do you really think this is the best way? I could help you back on your feet maybe. We could look into getting you some outreach help. There are agencies who can assist with the sort of problems you're facing..."

"I don't mean to be rude, June, but I have no time for, or faith in, your agencies. I have rejected the constricting grasp of such bureaucratic behemoths. They are inhuman and exist only to feed upon themselves and those of us who fall beneath their talons. And now, you have to go. Someone would like to speak with me, but he will not approach as long as you are here."

Roddy looks past me to the tunnel entrance. The fine hairs on the back of my neck stand up and I feel goose bumps on my arms. I turn to see who he's talking about and expect some apparition straight from the most twisted part of my subconscious. All along the platform are end of day commuters, briefcases and umbrellas in hand, sensible shoes, raincoats, jeans and leather jackets. I see no one who qualifies as a tunnel dweller.

"I don't see anyone, Roddy."

"Nevertheless, he is there. I must ask you to go. Quickly, quickly."

I still can't see anyone coming, but Roddy seems insistent and so, dismissed like a student from the head master's office, I stand up and say good-bye. I get on the next train and as it pulls out of the station I catch a glimpse of a small man, not badly dressed, chinos and a Manchester rugby shirt. He seems to be approaching Roddy,... but then the train picks up speed and we are gone.

I sit on a cushion, pure silk cream with tufted corners, which serves as a chair in my room. On the slate table before me is a wooden bowl holding smooth round pebbles. I take a small stone in my hand and feel soothed by the satiny polished texture. I put it in my mouth and feel it warming under my tongue. The room is quiet and still.

It is a long night. I sit on the cushion until the dark settles in around me. I rise to turn on a soft light behind a paper screen. I sit on the window seat. I look out across the night sky and the stars and try to find my place in relation to them. I seek to navigate through the obsidian pitch to some fixed point of light. Everything is ether and dark.

My rooms take on the look of luxury to my eyes. So much tranquillity, so much air. A glass bowl of star fruit sits on the

counter in the kitchen, never to be eaten, but because their daffodil stem colour is pleasing against the wooden counter. Above
the bed is a Japanese watercolour, understated and perfect. Everything is precise and chosen for effect on eye and spirit. What I
once believed to be austere now looks merely affluent.

I go back, my guilt a cashmere stole across my shoulders,
to look for Roddy. I travel to the Church Street Subway wishing
the train were faster, then wishing it were slower. I am shy again,
with my decision so poised and gifted.

I smile and raise my gaze, expectant in my magnanimity.

My eyes are empty as though sun-blind for a moment, because before me are only tiles, polished a gaudy spotless orange. Roddy is not here. There is no evidence. Perhaps the faint
cat-scratch smell of urine, nothing more. I stand, a stupid heavy
thing in the gush of human traffic, awash in the movement of
bodies. I sit down on the Roddy-empty ledge and put my ungloved
hand palm-down on the tile, hunting for warmth in this cold
place. There is no residue or vibration. He is re-absorbed somehow into the stomach of the city. I watch the subways come and
go, a rhythm like the pumping of blood through the veins, like
the movement of matter through bowel. I look for a scrap of
plastic, a button maybe, something which would be precious
only to Roddy but which would indicate his possible return. I am
caught by some script, tiny and discreet, scratched through the
paint of the pillar beside the ledge. Letters scraped through to
reveal metal bright below. I twist myself to read the lines. I cannot. I twist some more until I am lying down, my head close to
the pillar. I feel like a prisoner in a cell, a hard bunk, no pillow
for my head, apart from all of my kind. I read the words etched
in a trim hand.

> Ample make this bed.
> Make this bed with awe;
> In it wait till judgement break
> Excellent and fair.

> Be its mattress straight,
> Be its pillow round;
> Let no sunrise' yellow noise
> Interrupt this ground.

It is a poem by Emily Dickinson.

I walk to the end of the platform, peering down the dark tunnel for signs of my friend. I am too afraid to enter that labyrinth and look for him. I am afraid I wouldn't find him. I am afraid I would and he wouldn't come with me. I am afraid he would. I realise I am standing with both hands clasped over my mouth. A train approaches in from the blackness, all bright lights and noise. I step back until I am against the wall. The air rushes in first, then the bone-screech of metal against metal as the brakes work. Then the platform is full of people. I don't move until five or six trains have come and gone. Then I too move along the platform, up the stairs and out into the boisterous day.

It is many months before I realise that one morning I climbed the stairs from the subway to the street and I didn't look for Roddy.

The Kind Of Time You End Up With

Devon sat Carla down on the couch.

"Sit still," he said, "just listen."

"Fine."

"Just give it a chance, OK?"

"Yes. Fine."

He put the needle down on the record's groove. Crackle. Pop. The record had seen a lot of use over the years.

"Close your eyes," he said.

"Devon..."

"Go on."

As Hendrix's guitar rolled in Devon closed his eyes too.

There must be some kinda way outta here
Said the joker to the thief...

"Isn't that great?" Devon rolled his head back, playing air guitar. The corners of his mouth pulled down, his lower lip stuck out. Hendrix, man. Hendrix was a god.

...There's too much confusion
I can't get no relief...

Devon opened his eyes and looked at Carla. A couple of weeks back he'd been in the boxing gym, training for next week's match, and decided to stop into The Magic Garden, the restaurant on Grace Street where everybody was hanging out these days. She was coming out and waving goodbye to some friends, not watching where she was going. Before he could stop her, she smashed into him and bounced off his chest like a bird off a plate glass window. He just barely caught hold of her before she fell. She was so light he thought her bones must surely be hollow.

"Whoa there!" he said, a steadying arm around her waist, another at her wrist.

"I'm so sorry, I wasn't looking," she said, slightly dazed, her voice the sound of warm honey. She tossed her head and blinked a couple of times. She wore a loose sleeveless dress the colour of amethyst with silver earrings and bracelets. Her eyes were the same colour as her dress. She put one hand on his neck and the other in his palm. She smiled and looked up at him. "Shall we dance?"

She was so delicate he felt like an over-muscled gorilla, but he didn't want to let her go. Being careful not to stumble, Devon dipped her, the bumps of her spine a string of pearls under his fingers, and raised her up again. She laughed delightedly.

"Let me buy you a glass of wine. To say sorry," he said.

"But I'm the one who crashed into you. And besides, I was leaving."

"So don't leave. Stay."

And to his surprise, she did.

Carla was not, he kept telling himself, the most beautiful woman he'd ever been with, but there was something about her he couldn't get out of his head. He wanted to get next to her. Wanted her to get under his skin. He'd never felt like that before. The women he usually hung out with were what he called Leather Skirt Girls. Women who hung around the gym and the fights. High heels. Tight blouses. Lots of mascara. Red mouths. Girls who knew what the score was and didn't expect much. Girls with a bit of rough.

Carla wasn't like that. Carla was silky smooth. Her shoulder length hair was fair and so light the faintest breeze lifted it and set it dancing. Her waist was so small he could almost span it with his hands and as supple as a river reed from years of ballet. She painted her toenails pink. Her breasts were small and high.

She listened to Dylan and Joni Mitchell. Said she didn't get Hendrix.

Sometime during this afternoon, when they'd sat talking on the Garden's terrace, Carla sipping Assam tea and Devon with a beer, he realised it had become crucially important to him that she like Hendrix. She'd agreed to come back to his apartment.

...Let us not talk falsely now,
The hour's getting late ...

She sat on the edge of his old brown plaid couch, and as she listened to the melody her hands moved in the air, making shapes as though spinning the notes into pattern. Her lips were parted slightly. She smiled.

Two riders were approaching
And the wind began to howl...

She opened her eyes.

"Yes," she said. "Yes." He let out the air he'd been holding in his lungs. "I admit it, it's amazing."

They listened to every Hendrix album he had, and he had them all. When she went home he waited an hour then he dialled her number.

"Hello?" she said.

He didn't know what he wanted to say.

"Hello?"

He hung up, feeling like a fool. But he'd just wanted to hear her voice.

A month later Carla was in Beth's kitchen, watching her chop tomatoes for puttanesca sauce. Beth was a big girl, with short cut hair, the colour, this week, of raspberries. She wore rings on every finger and her thumbs as well and said exactly what she pleased, whenever she pleased. She was honest and blunt and didn't have a tactful bone in her body. Even though they were both only twenty-two, Carla had always felt as though

Lauren B. Davis

Beth was older, more worldly wise. They'd been best friends since high school. Two nights before Carla had brought Devon to Beth's party, so he could meet her friends.

"I don't understand what you see in him, that's all," said Beth.

"Well, for one thing, he's gorgeous."

"I suppose so, if you like the brooding black Irish type. Very Heathcliff. But Jesus, a boxer? How long do you suppose he'll stay gorgeous? "

"He's very good. You should come see him fight sometime."
"I don't think so."

"Snob."

"No. Just too senseless for me. And for you too, I would have thought," said Beth, scraping the tomatoes into a cast iron pot. "Unless, of course, it's the primitive sex that's enthralling you."

"Did you even talk to him? Did you know he's planning on being a cop?"

"I thought we'd start with the boxing shit and work our way down."

"Meaning?"

"Meaning cops are a less evolved species even than boxers. The two together is a combination that makes me queasy. I can't see it, Carla. What do you talk about?"

"Music. Our dreams. He wants to get a cabin up in the hills. Build it himself."

"Carla, you are a choreographer. You are a city girl. A woman of the arts. You are not George of the Jungle's mountain mate."

"He makes me feel special."

"You *are* special. You don't need him to make you feel that."

"He makes me feel... I don't know...cherished, protected, like we belong together."

"Oh for God's sake!" Beth laughed. "Don't tell me you're in love with this big slab of meat?"

"I think I am."

Beth groaned and Carla threw a piece of parsley at her.

"Don't look like that. It's hard to explain. I think about him

98

all the time. He's just so different from the men I've been with. He's so fully a *man!* And he treats me like I'm made out of glass. I just want to curl up next to him all the time. I know, this doesn't sound like me. He makes me want to be taken care of. But he's not fawning over me all the time. Sometimes I'm not sure I even know where I stand with him."

"And that's good?"

"No. Yes. It's like he's withholding a part of himself, like he's got a secret place. You know? It makes him more interesting. It's addictive."

"You're in for trouble girl, I'm telling you."

"I don't care," said Carla. "I just don't care."

"You will."

One night several months later Carla and Devon went to a party given by three of his friends, Mick, Danny and Richard, who lived together in a big run-down house on Larchmont Street. The kitchen was full of beer and vodka shooters. The music blared from the open windows, and more than one person threw up across the fence into the neighbour's yard.

Carla was not enjoying herself. Devon was drinking far too much. He did that now and then. Not every night, but too much. She knew a few years ago, when he was barely twenty, he'd had a problem with speed, but he promised her he'd kicked it. No needles, he said. Never again. But she didn't like it when he drank this way, inhaling tequila like the only point in life was to reach that worm at the bottom of the bottle.

They'd been there a couple of hours. She wanted to go home.

"I'm going to the bathroom, Devon. Then can we go?"

"We just got here," he said, taking a swig from the mescal bottle he'd picked up in the kitchen.

"Please."

"Go to the can, Babe, then we'll see." He turned her and patted her behind, which she hated. "Go on."

Carla had to wait ten minutes until the couple in the lone bathroom finished doing whatever it was they were doing in there. They came out, rumpled and flushed, the man wiping his nose, the woman sniffling and bright-eyed.

"Sorry," the girl mumbled.

"Took our time, huh," said the man. "How about I make it up to you, you want a line?"

"No, I want the toilet," she said and pushed past them.

When she came back to the living room, Devon was nowhere in sight. She wandered through the clumps of bodies, looking for him, feeling out of place and disjointed in the dim light and bone-vibrating sound. As she passed the room from where the music came, she heard Devon's familiar "Yahoo!" and followed the sound of his voice. She stood in the doorway and watched, a sick feeling in her stomach.

He sat on a kitchen chair in the middle of the otherwise nearly bare room, his legs wide spread, balanced backwards and tilted. Two men slouched against the wall, cigarettes dangling, their faces hidden in shadow. A girl stood between then, blonde hair wild and teased high. She had her hand on the crotch of the shorter man's pants. Another girl with heavy thighs and a round high backside danced in front of Devon. She wore a very short tight skirt and a midriff-baring orange blouse with the top buttons undone. She pushed her thick black hair up to the top of her head and waggled her bottom in his face. Her skirt rode up, revealing white panties beneath. Then she turned and put her hands under her fleshy breasts and pushed them up, rolling her belly and shoulders. She caught sight of Carla standing in the doorway and smiled at her, slow and self-satisfied.

"Yahoo!" Devon hollered again.

She walked up behind him and touched his shoulder.

"Devon," she said, icily, "I'm going."

"Hey Baaaby! You gonna dance?" His sky-coloured eyes were shiny and narrow. He grabbed her arm and pulled her down to his lap. She struggled, furious to get away from him. The shadow men against the wall laughed.

"Don't! Let me go. I want to go home." She dug her nails into his arm and he let her go. She started to cry.

"Hey, don't let me stop you," he said. The dancing girl rolled her hips. Carla fled from the room.

As she reached the car, he was right behind her. He put his arms around her, buried his face in her hair.

"Sorry," he whispered.

"You humiliated me." She was shaking.

"That's nothing in there. Nothing. She's just a party girl. You shouldn't get so upset."

"You shouldn't act like a vulgar fool."

"Take me home, darlin'." His hands moved over her belly in slow circles. "You know you're the only woman in the world I love. Take me home."

Her knees went weak and soft licks of flame moved up the inside of her thighs. He was a wild man, but he loved her, only her. He was going home with her.

Three months later, he said he wanted to live with her. She cleared out dresser drawers, made room for his clothes in her closet, his collection of records and his beaten-up old leather chair. She was sure that once they were in the same house he would quiet down. He was taking this huge step. He would be hers completely.

As they lay in bed that night, Devon watched Carla sleep, the slanted light from the blinds bringing lines of her fine pale body into sharp relief. He vowed right then and there to protect her from all the unclean, unkind things in the world. She looked so vulnerable, so untainted by the shit he knew lurked around every corner. He would make money, build her a fine life. He'd be a cop who lived up to the code of honour. He'd live up to her vision of him. He'd put the darkness behind him. He could do it.

He pulled her close to his belly, his hand cupping her small breast. In her sleep she moved to hold his hand, but it was far too large so she wrapped her fingers around his thumb and held on to that.

Devon's boxing coach was named Gaston. He was a tough little French Quebecer, missing two fingers from his right hand, a souvenir from a dispute with some unnamed men in dark suits over a promising fighter some years before. At no more than five foot four, he had spent years bullying boxers into shape. He was universally respected and obeyed without question. One of his many rules was that the fighters' girlfriends were forbidden from coming to the bouts. He said it put the boxers at a disadvantage.

"It's no good, eh? The girls, they come down, eh, and then they get crazy the first time they see blood. Me, I ain't gonna have my fighters worried about their little twinkies. No distractions, eh? Keep your mind on the fight! *Tabernac!*" With every third or fourth word his chin jutted as though daring someone to take a punch at him.

Gaston didn't like anybody. He was famous for it. But he liked Carla. For Carla he made an exception. When the other boxers complained he simply replied, "Hey, my gym, my rules. You don't like it, go find Don King."

Devon felt like the champion of the world when she sat ringside and Gaston knew it. Devon would destroy anyone who tried to make him look bad in front of this girl. It was through Carla that Gaston found Devon's killer instinct. Carla would wear something nice. A dress, high heels. She had her lipstick on and perfume. She never even flinched when Devon got hit, when he bled. Neither did she scream out encouragement. She sat, a calm pool of grace in a rumble of fight fans. Devon's opponents knew she wasn't afraid of him getting hit and that made them think he was invincible. As she waited for the bell to ring, Carla wound up hand wraps. When she had a tight coil in her palm, she let it unroll and started to wind again.

That year he took home the Golden Gloves Silver Medal and she had it framed and hung it on their bedroom wall.

She became traditional. She cooked dinners and wore scraps of flimsy lace in the bedroom. He came home from the police academy on weekends, tired and worn out. She rubbed his bunched muscles. Quizzed him on the law. Her friends despaired. His friends became frequent visitors at their small apartment. He liked to show her off, let his old buddies see how good he had it, how fine she was, how he'd landed on his feet at last. He threw himself into the role of provider and protector as though holding onto a floating spar in a tossed sea. He cut down on the booze, did no drugs. He stayed home nights when he wasn't training for the force.

He couldn't wait to be a cop.

The day he got his badge, stood straight and tall in the rigid rows, he knew he'd be all right. Knew he'd found a righteous path. Carla sat in the audience, clapping so hard her hands were red, tears mixing with laughter as the pride burst out. They were going to make it.

Beth sat next to her and rolled her eyes.

Carla snapped photos with her little black camera, had them developed and hung them on the wall next to his silver boxing medal.

As they settled into a routine, however, Devon became more and more plagued by restlessness. He told her they should get out more, go dancing, go hear a band. So they went dancing and if at times she got her feelings hurt, as he flirted with other women at the bar, other women on the dance floor, she didn't say so.

He wore her out. She didn't want to be running the streets every night he wasn't working. She missed their quiet times to-gether, sharing a bowl of pasta, a glass of wine, a bubble bath and candle-fuelled conversation. She didn't like the places he liked. They were too dark, too smoky, too filled with people who were unmistakably on the opposite side of the law from the one to which he professed dedication.

He was newly a police officer but he seemed more at home with people he was likely to have to arrest one day than with their neighbours or friends.

He seemed pulled in two directions and she didn't know how to win the tug of war.

"I gotta go out. It's too cooped up in this place," he said, night after night.

"You go," she finally said, "I'm too tired."

"You sure?"

"Yes."

"I'd like you to come with me."

"No," she said, wishing he would stay but afraid to sound

Lauren B. Davis

like a nag, "you go if you want to. I don't mind."

And he went. He ambled down to Prince Street, past the hookers leaning into car windows, their fleshy wares goose-pimpled in the cold night.

"Ladies," he said and touched his forehead in a gentleman's salute.

"Awful cold out here tonight, *Officer,*" said a girl in a rabbit fur jacket, effortlessly identifying him as what he was. "Care to warm up someplace?"

"Not tonight, sugar, my lady's got a light left on for me back home."

"So what you doing out here?" she challenged, her teeth white in her thin dark face.

He went into Palomino's, the strip club on Harbour Square. He leaned against the bar, his foot cocked up on the rail, a beer in one hand, tequila shooter on the side. He watched the girls dance in the black light, their skin like cream, the white of their g-string snippets electric icing on pubic mounds and buttocks. He started to get an erection.

A buxom brunette with nothing on but a string, pasties and high heels came over to him and placed her hand on his arm. She squeezed his muscle appreciatively.

"Hi there," she said, her lips glossy and sticky, "how you doing tonight?"

"Just fine. Just fine."

"How about a table dance?"

Her round hard breasts stuck out at an angle so precise it could only be obtained with plastic. He had the urge to jiggle them up and down, see if they'd move.

"No thanks."

"How about buying me a drink?"

"Sure." He signalled the waiter. She ordered a champagne cocktail and when it came stirred it with a long white fingernail.

"We've got a room in the back. Maybe you'd like a lap dance?"

"Don't think so."

"You sure?"

104

"Yup. That's not what I want."

"Oh? Well, what do you want?"

He leaned over and whispered in her ear. "I'm looking for the candy store."

"Ah. A pharmacist, huh?" She smiled. She had lipstick on her upper teeth. "Don't go anywhere. I'll talk to Rita. Be right back." She ran her finger along his lips. "Then maybe we can persuade you to play a little."

"Maybe."

The girl disappeared. Devon's heart beat fast. He knocked down the tequila. He shouldn't be doing this. This wasn't what he had planned. If Carla ever found out... but she loved him... she understood him. She wouldn't find out. *Don't be an asshole, Devon. You'll break her heart.* He didn't even know how he'd ended up in this joint. He hadn't intended to come here. He'd meant to go to the Garden, see if some of the guys were around. It wasn't too late. He could still leave.

He could see the brunette come through a back door, a big greasy smile on her face, another woman, shorter, older, thicker, following behind. Before they got to him he reached into his pocket, tossed a couple of bills on the bar and bolted.

"You're back quick," said Carla, the relief on her face evident. She sat in bed with a book, one of his old sweaters over her pyjamas. He just knew she had a pair of thick socks on her tiny dancer's feet. She always had cold feet.

He threw himself on the bed, pulled down the covers and rubbed his face on her stomach. She smelled of freshly ironed sheets and the sandalwood she used in her bath water.

"I missed you," he said. She stroked his head until he fell asleep.

He'd been a cop about a year. He was out on the streets all night long, stepping in the filth of the city, getting it in his pores, up his nostrils. The slug end of humanity rolled up in a tidal wave on every shift. It made him sick, and yet, it fascinated him. All that money, all that dope, all that dirty sex right there under your nose for the taking. He began staying out with the other cops, hanging out at cop bars. It was part of the game. You had to kick it with your partner, shake off the shit so you didn't track it in the house.

He began staying out even when he wasn't at the cop bar.

Carla didn't like it. Said he was changing. Said she could see the fingerprints of other women on his skin. She spent long evenings talking with Beth, crying over how remote he'd become, how they were drifting.

"I won't say it," said Beth, biting back an I-told-you-so.

"Don't. I love him."

"You ever heard of that experiment with the rats? Well, it goes like this: three rats in three cages, right? They each have these little pedal things that they're supposed to press to get a food pellet. OK, so the first rat, when he presses it, he always gets a pellet so he learns to press it only when he's hungry, sure there'll always be enough. The second rat, he presses the pedal but never gets a pellet, so he gives up and ignores the thing. But the third rat, ah, the third rat, he presses the pedal and sometimes gets a pellet and sometimes doesn't, so what does he do? He stands there pressing that pedal over and over again until he goes nuts and his little paw falls off."

"And?"

"I suggest, my soggy friend, you are the third rat. Victim of random gratification. Dev loves you sometimes and doesn't love you others and sometimes he's good, he's very, very good and sometimes he's so bad he's rotten. And you're a junkie for this guy."

"But God, Beth, when it's just the two of us, together, it can be so amazing. He wants to be a good man. I know that."

"So what's stopping him? Why's he treating you like shit?"

"He's afraid of something."

"He should be afraid, he should be very afraid, but I suspect he's not, the asshole."

She grew thinner and she clung to him tighter. He didn't like it.

"What I do on my time is my business," he'd say.

"Be careful 'your' time isn't the only kind of time you end up with," she'd reply and the shadows under her eyes got darker. "I can't take much more of this, Devon. You've got to take better care of me than this. You've got to take better care of us."

She drew lines in the sand saying, "This far and no further." Their passion kept blurring the lines though, and he didn't think she was looking too closely to see if they'd been crossed.

He was wrong.

A year later, she was the One That Got Away.

He screwed it up. He knew that. But he loved her. She should have hung in there. They had history. That should have been worth something.

He got drunk and had her name tattooed on his shoulder with a bright red broken heart. When they saw it the guys at the station laughed at him, but not to his face, because he was getting a reputation for someone who'd fly off the handle, who couldn't control his temper. His partner, Joe Maccio, told him he better cut back on the coke.

He had a studio apartment a block from Thief in the Night, the cop bar where he hung out. Late at night he sat on a folding lawn chair looking out at the Chinese Laundry across the street. The same film kept running over and over in front of his eyes. He could still see her face.

"I warned you, Devon. I said that if I ever found you cheating on me again, I'd be gone. No screaming, no crying, just gone." But she was crying. Heavy tears in lines down her face. "I hope she was worth it."

If she had yelled at him, if she had hit him, he would have felt better, and found a way to get his arms around her. But she didn't. She just stood there with the tears making her face shine and her eyes sparkle. He had nothing to say.

There had been other women before. Carla had accused him of wearing them like flags around his neck. She said she'd grown so she could hear the scritch-scratch of another woman's nails along his skin from miles away. He'd laughed at her. Told her to stop being so melodramatic, it wasn't what she thought.

And it hadn't been. She should have known that. He would always have come home to her. It was just that he got twisted up inside sometimes and he needed to go and get a little low-down. It felt good to roll around out in the dark now and then. Let loose the beast a little. There were things she wouldn't understand, things he didn't want her to understand, things he wanted to keep separate from her. Why couldn't she just have let him do that?

He poured another shot of tequila. The tears came. He howled until his throat bled.

She'd be back. She'd punish him for a while, that was to be expected. But she'd get over it. He sat outside her apartment in a taxi, letting the meter click away. He sent flowers to her at work. He started turning up at her office, in that arty warehouse down on Richmond, full of faggy dancers. He hung out in the reception area at quitting time. Then one day the security guard asked him, politely but firmly, not to come back any more. He pushed the fat fuck over a low table, flat on his ass. What did they think he was? He was a fucking cop!

She phoned his lieutenant, complained. Asked them to do something. He got a warning. The lieutenant told him to cool it.

She didn't need to do that. She wanted to be left alone? Fine. He'd leave her alone.

For about six months he did just that. Then, he called her. She talked to him on the phone, like he knew she would. She was still close. He persuaded her to meet for a coffee.

She was prettier than ever. But she wouldn't stay.

"Devon, look, I'm only here because I want to tell you face to face. This is over. We're not getting back together. I'll always care about you, but you're too messed up for me. You've got too many problems. Do you understand?"

He understood. She behaved as though she didn't want to get involved with him again, but he knew it was an act. It was only a matter of time. About a year later, he started driving by her house again. Just sitting out front, looking in the window at her and the new guy she was living with. He could tell by the way they sat, so far from each other at opposite ends of the couch, that it'd never work out.

He started calling her and not saying anything. Just to hear her voice.

Two years later he got tossed off the force. Bastards. Unsuitable. Mental problems. All that shit. What did they know? OK, maybe he shouldn't have popped Johnson, but hey, he had it coming. Accusing him of being a dirty cop. Should have killed the little fucker. And that bit about unnecessary force... Fuck them. Fuck them all.

Nobody understood loyalty any more. Loyalty for life. You made pledges, you kept them. That's what friendship was supposed to be about and cops were supposed to stick together. Like real love. It should mean forever.

He needed money, a guy had to live, so he went back to fighting, but only temporary. No more Golden Gloves, no time for professional bouts. He needed money fast. Club fighting. It wouldn't be for long. A couple more months, until something turned up, security work, or bodyguarding for some famous actress or something. Definitely no longer than the new year.

He was pretty good at fighting though. He could walk away with $5,000 a night if he was in form and hadn't been hitting the booze or the coke too hard the day before. Club fighting was a hard game. Bare knuckles, few rules. Usually he wore a mouth guard, but he'd lost it last night and now he had a hole in his chin to show for it. He fought for fat, pasty, jaded men who dug the contact high produced by the illegal nature of the bouts and the equally illegal high stakes betting. He fought best when he was angry and he got angry more and more easily.

These brawlers he was fighting, they had no honour. A real boxer had honour; it was a clean, righteous sport. But these guys didn't care about that. They'd tear an ear off, Tyson-style, or try and take you out with a shot to the balls.

He had to be careful of his left. He'd torn his rotator cuff in a car accident a while back and then a few months ago he'd ripped it up again. It'd been stupid and his fault, he shouldn't have fought as hung over and full of the jangles as he'd been, but he'd needed the money. He'd shot out with a clear left jab, or so he'd thought, but he'd overextended and the Sasquatch he'd been fighting had dealt him a crippling long, hard right just where the muscle connected to the rotator. Put his whole left out of commission. He couldn't summon the strength to keep his shoulder up and protect himself. The pain had been like having a muscle full of broken glass, nearly blinding him every time he took a shot. He was left wide open, exposed. He'd connected with a lucky right cross himself and taken the bastard out soon after, thank God, but still, the left side of his face had been pretty messed up. The shoulder was mostly healed now, but he had to watch it. You lost your left and you were out of the game permanently.

And the crowds. God, how he hated the crowds. The bouts were held in blind pigs late at night. He felt like a stripper, naked, just a piece of meat. A lot of the time there wasn't even a ring, just a roped off area on the floor, slippery with cigarette butts and spilled beer. He'd been spit on, had bottles and lit cigars thrown at him. Sometimes there was a net up to protect the fighters from the fans, but that was rare.

He won more than he lost. He could take a punch and keep on going. Then his opponent would do something that would piss him off, take a cheap shot or go beyond the bounds Devon thought permissible when they were locked up and dealing out trash talk. Some things a man had no right to say to another man, even if he was trying to intimidate an opponent. You didn't talk about a man's past, about what he'd lost. Generally a man only overstepped that mark once. Word was out that Devon was crazy, and that was fine with him. He'd go blind with anger and when the curtain of rage lifted, the other guy was on the floor. So he'd be a hero for a while, letting the guys who'd won big betting on him buy him drinks and hookers.

It was a hard game though, and he didn't know how much longer he'd be able to last. And, if the truth be told, he was lonely. Plain old, cold-house, empty-bed lonely. It wasn't supposed to be like this. It wasn't at all what he'd planned. A man shouldn't be alone. A man should have kids and a woman. Someone you could phone up in the middle of the day saying, "Take a bubble bath, baby, and put on your red dress. I'm taking you out tonight!" Someone who was a lady in public and something else entirely behind closed doors.

It had been a hard night. A hard fight.

Devon lay on the bed, letting the darkness soothe him. He could feel the nagging tingle begin. It was familiar and he knew it would grow. He didn't want to make the call. He could keep it in control. Just let the soft dark quiet him down. Breathe. He didn't mean to keep thinking about her, but it often happened this way, in the deep tangled pit of a night like this one. It wasn't something he would admit to anyone. But Carla would understand. They were connected in that way. That was their secret - how they were connected to each other in something older, more profound than could be explained in words. They were marrow-deep.

The room was dark; the only light trickled in the door from the fluorescent fixture over the kitchen sink. The bed floated like a garbage scow surrounded by the pollution of abandoned grey gym socks, Everlast boxing trunks, high top running shoes, Levi's, a couple of black T-shirts, a leather shoe, rumpled shirts. There were also empty bottles of Johnny Walker and mescal, Domino pizza boxes, cans of Colt and overflowing ashtrays. The sheets felt greasy. He hadn't made the bed in weeks. He was wearing only his underwear. The sweatshirt he'd been wearing, stained with drops of blood, was lying on the floor, discarded alongside his jeans and running shoes. He held a towel with several ice cubes in it, alternating between the bone over his left eye, where a shot glass-size knot had formed, and his mouth, which was also swollen and had a hole in it where his left incisor had cut through his bottom lip. He could probably use a stitch there. Next to the bed was a nightstand table on which stood a bottle of tequila and a bowl of rosy-tinted ice water in which he periodically soaked his hands.

He didn't think he'd broken anything, although he'd be pissing blood tomorrow. He reached over into the nightstand drawer and popped open the lid on a bottle of painkillers. He

Lauren B. Davis

poured a few pills into his mouth, chewed them up and washed
them down with a gulp of tequila, wincing as the oily liquid
seared into the ragged inside of his mouth. He raised the bottle to
his lips a second time and swallowed, then swallowed again,
and again. He didn't seem to be able to get drunk.

On his stomach lay the phone. His hands were sweaty
against the cold grey plastic.

The bittersweet guitar caress of *Little Wing* wove across the
room and his eyes came to rest on the poster of Hendrix on the
wall at the foot of the bed. Taken from the cover of the *War He-
roes* album, it showed Jimi's face close up, real close up. So
close you could see the pain in his eyes, how he had a premoni-
tion he was going to die young. You could see his loneliness.
Hendrix was genius, no doubt about it. Devon's mind floated
along the thread the music played out. He drifted a little, away
from the pain slicing like a blunt razor through his kidneys and
his head.

A man shouldn't have to live the way he'd been living.
There was only one person who'd understand that. Maybe she
was thinking about him right now. Devon lifted the receiver from
the phone and dialled the number. It rang four times and then he
heard her voice.

"Hello?" She sounded all sleepy and warm, just like she
was right there beside him.   "Hello?...Hello?..Oh for God's
sake!" Click.

She knew it was him, he could tell.

He reached down and put his hand around himself. He was
already swollen and hard. With the sound of her voice still in his
ears, he provided himself with what comfort he could, and when
he was finished, pulled up the sheet and hoped his aching body
would let him sleep.

Harold Luddock's Decision

The problem with death is not the being dead, it's the getting there, the dying. That's what I say. It's a messy business, and undignified. I'm old enough to know I don't want to live forever. Don't even really want to live another year, truth be known. I seen enough to know the world isn't going to improve any and I'm not going to either. After eighty it's all pretty much down hill, is what I'm thinking. Liver, stomach, joints, eyes, goddamn bladder... I hurt in all the places where I used to play, if you catch my meaning. Spend half the night in the goddamn john with nothing to show for it except another sleepless night.

No, I'm ready to be dead. I'm just fed up with getting there is all. Doctors say there's nothing much they can do unless I want to undergo all that chemo crap. And I do not, no sir, I do not. Can't think of a single good reason to spend my last few months on earth with my stomach inside out and what little hair I have left in a heap on the floor. Wouldn't make much difference in the long run, now would it? And if they did fix me, which they won't, 'cause even they admit things are too far along for that, they'd only be getting rid of this just so's I can die of something else the week after. Don't make no sense at all. 'Sides, I don't like hospitals. Never did. No, I'd prefer to die in the place of my choosin', on my own terms, just the same way's I've lived my life. My own terms.

Have to admit, I always did like to get my own way 'bout things. Used to drive Maggie to distraction. She said I was the most contrary man ever to draw breath and she was sure I'd live to a ripe old age because the good Lord wouldn't be able to stand my company any more'n anyone else could. He sure wouldn't rush bringing me home. Yup, well, must explain why she died when she did. Woman sure was a pleasure, in every way a man could want. Ah well, ah well, never mind, no, never mind. Long time passed. And it won't be long now, no, won't be long at all.

But it's the getting there that's sure a pain in the ass. Everybody tiptoeing around you like you was the first one ever to come down with a case of the terminals. Harold Jr. can't barely look me in the eye and Cindy, his wife, keeps wanting to hug me all the time, for crissake. All I want to do is get up in the mountain where the air's clean and quiet, away from the ministrations of those two and all these people wanting to keep visiting, see how I am. Neighbours in and out all the time. Folk I never even thought of as friends suddenly crawling out the woodwork, trying to "ease" my days. Each thinking they're going to be the one to save me. God help me. Morbid old biddies most of 'em, clacking around the house with their tuna casseroles and prayer books.

Just get me up there on the high ground with Daisy and my rifle and do me a little hunting. At least the dog don't treat me any different. But Cindy decided I was too sick to be heading up the mountain by myself. What the hell does she think's going to happen? I might die? Well, I'm gonna take care of that and head out early in the morning before her skinny city butt's even out of bed. I don't hardly sleep no more anyhow, so it won't be no hardship for me to be out before the sun's up.

Don't know why she and Harold had to move back in anyway. But they did and now I can't get rid of them. I know they mean well, but I'm just not used to all the fussing. They shoulda had children of their own, them two. Give 'em something to take care of other than this stringy old rooster. I can't abide being fussed over and if I don't take matters in hand, well, soon I'm not going to be able to shake 'em off. They're good kids, don't mean to say they're not, and they'll take good care of the place when I'm gone, but it's enough to make anyone squirrelly, somebody always trying to stick a pill down your throat or wrap you up in blankets like a goddamn newborn.

Maybe it's the pain that makes me so ornery, but they sure are standing on my last nerve. And that medicine the doctor gave me to "manage" the pain, as he said, sure ain't doing the trick like before.

No, I'm gonna take my dog and head up the mountain, up to where I can see a good long way off, with nothing standing in the way of the sky and me. My old legs'll carry me up there still, and if I reckon I don't have enough left in me to get back down, well, Daisy'll find her way home all right.

Lauren B. Davis

Cat's Out Of The Bag

She'd only gone over to feed the neighbour's cat. God bless the Swansons for going away on weekends and leaving sweet, reliable Annie to take care of their precious Minouche. She'd told her husband Larry she'd only be gone a couple of minutes. And of course, he'd trusted her, so she'd have to be quick. Quick to feed the fat hairball writhing around her legs. Quick to spoon out chunks of meaty swill into a plastic dish. Quick to the Swanson's liquor cabinet. Quick to the bottle of vodka, which wouldn't leave too much of a smell on her breath. Quick to gulp down a few mouthfuls. Wait just a few seconds. Take another drink, and let it flow, warm and golden flowing down inside, melting all the bad spots. The switch in her head flipped. Lovely switch. Friendly, happy switch. The little voice said, *don't ever let me stop feeling this way, don't ever let me come down. Don't lose the velvet caress. Take a wee drop more.*

The problem was, she'd gone one swig of the bottle too far. It was so treacherous, one tiny step and, oops! She should have stopped a couple of mouthfuls ago, when she still would have been steady on her feet, undetectable in the bubble of vodka bliss.

But it might be all afternoon before she could excuse herself to get back to check on the cat again. It had to be enough to last. One more.

Her stomach bounced. She put the bottle back in the cupboard, went into the bathroom and found the toothpaste. She put a dollop on the end of her tongue and chewed it around long enough to cover up any telltale liquor fumes. She rinsed her mouth and spat in the bowl. She raised her head and the room tilted. She fluffed her curly hair. She patted her face with cool water. She looked flushed. She giggled. Bright eyes. Pretty bright eyes.

On the way back to their house she dropped the keys and had to be careful not to wobble when she bent over to pick them up. Deliberate movements were best. She decided she'd start to make lunch right away. Soup. Soup would entail lots of chopping and stirring which would occupy her while the booze levelled out in her veins.

Larry was out back, lying in the hammock, reading the Saturday paper. He was a big bear of a man, not fat, but with a solidness to him. His legs were like stone columns. His chest was pelted and broad.

"Hey ho! Just me," she called out.

"Cat OK?"

"But of course, darhrling" she used her Boris and Natasha accent. "I think I'll make minestrone for lunch. How's that sound?"

"Oh, I don't care. Hey, come here, you." Larry opened his arms out to her, inviting her to the hammock for a cuddle.

"Can't right now, babe, gotta cook."

"Just for a minute."

"Hey, you want lunch or not?"

"I'd rather have you." He waggled his eyebrows up and down a few times.

"Later." She absolutely had to have a few minutes to get herself together. She slid closed the patio doors and turned to the 'fridge. She rummaged around for carrots and beans and tomatoes. Music. That's what this party needed. Annie walked into the living room and flipped John Mellencamp on the CD player. She turned the volume up loud. Singing along with the song she danced her way back into the kitchen. She did a little bump and grind and misjudged the distance. She hit the corner of the table, hard. The sharp impact sent a jolt of red pain into her hip. Ah well, another one of clumsy Annie's many mystery bruises.

"Shit! Shit! Shit!" She rubbed her hip.

"You all right?" Annie hadn't heard him come in.

"Yeah, just banged my hip. You know me!"

"Annie, look at me."

"What?"

"Have you been drinking?"

"Oh fine, every time I bump into something now, you're going to accuse me of being drunk!"

"I've seen you bump into enough stuff over the past couple of years, Annie."

"Look, we've been through this. We've talked it all out. We agreed I wouldn't have anything to drink unless it was a special occasion, right? Unless it was a birthday or we're on vacation or something, right?"

"That was the deal. No drinking behind my back. A glass of wine now and then, that's it. You agreed."

"Exactly. I agreed. So that's it. End of discussion."

"So you're saying you haven't had anything to drink."

"Are you calling me a liar?" She could feel the booze starting to shift around now. No longer the pretty, dancing honey in her limbs. Now it was treacle and dark. It was forming into balls of something not pretty, something angry. "Is that what you're trying to say?"

"I'll make this simple. Are you drunk? Tell me, Annie. I'm not fooling around."

"Of course I'm not drunk. For God's sake, it's 11 o'clock in the morning."

"I've seen you start earlier than this."

"Jesus, Larry. You're getting to be a bore, do you know that? A big fucking bore."

"You've been drinking. You think nobody can tell. You're wrong. You change, Annie."

"Lighten up, Larry." That sounded funny. Lighten up Larry,

like the name of one of their nephew's action figures. A superhero. She giggled. "Lighten-up Larry. That's what I'm going to call you from now on. Lighten-up Larry," she made a child's sing-song out of it. "Lighten-uuu-up Larry." It was a taunt.

Larry turned and walked out of the kitchen to the living room. He shut off the music. He stood looking out of the window onto the sunny bright street; watched his neighbours mow their lawns, wash their cars. He watched Jeff Parker push his daughter on her new bike, teaching her to balance and to ride.

Annie followed him in. She knew she should leave well enough alone, let it slide. He couldn't prove anything. But something in her wanted to push the envelope, get him to say he was wrong. She flipped on the music again. *Little pink houses for you and me...*

"What's with all the drama, Larry? I've told you I didn't drink anything. Told you that, right? What is your fucking problem!?!" She stood leaning back against the door jamb, her arms folded in front of her in a righteous pose.

Larry turned and looked at her. Annie tried to stare him down, but her eyes wandered a bit. She stuck her tongue out at him.

Larry sat down on the sofa. He dropped down like a person who's been punched in the stomach.

"Annie," he said, in a cracked voice, "I just don't feel like you're on my side any more." He put his head in his hands and hid himself from her.

"Not on your side...?" her voice trailed off. He was scaring her.

"No, Annie, not on my side. I don't know what to do. You're killing us. You're killing yourself. I can't trust you anymore. I can't tell you anything for fear you're going to blurt it out at some business dinner. You think you're being funny and make jokes about me in front of people who work for me. You think the employees at the company like you, but you're turning into a joke." His voice was rising, like he was calling to her over a great distance. "I'm afraid to include you in dinners when I take out clients. I'm afraid to take you to my family's place, because I'm always worried somebody's going to catch you in the kitchen sucking up the cooking sherry. I'm afraid to look in the back of the fucking closets because I don't want to find vodka bottles stashed there. You say you aren't drinking, but you are, of course you are. You're lying to me. I love you and I want to help you, but you're lying to me. I can't do this anymore. I can't be responsible for you. I can't trust you. I feel like I'm all alone here." His face was wet and his hands were clasped tightly in front of him as though he were afraid of what they might do if he let them move of their own volition.

"I need you," he said softly, "to be on my side. But right now, I don't think you're on anybody's side. Not even your own."

"Larry...I love you."

"I know. But it's just not enough to solve this."

And then she was crying. Really crying. She didn't want to be someone who turned against the one person she loved. She didn't want Larry to feel this way. She had made him feel this way. She was crying so hard that her muscles cramped up and her stomach heaved. She ran to the bathroom and vomited into the toilet. All the vodka, clear and lethal, flowed up like water from a backed-up sewer. After a few minutes the retching stopped and Annie sat on the bathroom floor. It was always the same after she puked, she was sober again, and she was filled with a horrible, painful shame.

He was right, of course. That was the terrible thing about it. She was on nobody's side anymore, except maybe Jack Daniels'. She was disgusting. She was a vile creature.

Annie rinsed her mouth. She looked at her face in the mirror. She was bloated. There were red spots on her face and neck where bloods vessels had broken. Her eyes were red and watery. Her mouth was loose, the lips looked rubbery. Larry always said she was beautiful. Clearly she wasn't the only one lying.

Annie came back into the living room. Larry hadn't moved.

"I'm so ashamed. Baby, I'm so sorry."

"You're always sorry. It doesn't help."

"I know. You're right. About everything. No more lies. I have been drinking. I practically drained the Swansons' liquor cabinet dry. I did that. It's like I can't stop myself. Jesus, I feel so humiliated." Her voice became choked and hoarse. "I don't know what's the matter with me." She was crying again.

Larry motioned for her to sit next to him on the sofa. He put his arm around her and she turned into his chest and sobbed.

"Yes, you do, Annie, you know exactly what the problem is."

"What are we going to do?"

"*We* aren't going to do anything. You are."

"OK," she said.

"OK," he said.

They sat holding onto each other for some minutes. Finally Larry pulled his arm away. He stood up and ran his hands over his face.

"So, what's it gonna be? No time like the present," he said.

"I said I'd do it. I will. What, you want me to do it right now?"

"Your decision."

"A day one way or the other isn't going to make a difference. Let's just have the weekend together."

"Fine."

Larry walked out of the room and reappeared a few minutes later with a sports bag slung over his shoulder.

"Where're you going?"

"I'm going to my brother's. I'll come back for some more clothes in a couple of days."

"What are you talking about? This is ridiculous. Don't be so dramatic."

"No more drama, Annie. When you get serious, when you get sober, you know where to find me."

He walked to the door, opened it and closed it behind him before she realised he meant it.

"Larry! Don't do this! Larry!" she yelled at the door.

It took a minute to register. She paused inside herself, wondering what she was going to do, whether she was going to cry or not. There weren't any tears. There was just a big black tar bubble of anger rising to the surface. *To hell with him! Where the fuck did he get off with this holier-than-thou attitude. Fuck him. Fuck him!*

"FUCK YOU FUCK YOU FUCK YOU FUCK YOU!"

Annie ran upstairs, down the hall, into the back bedroom and opened the closet. She grabbed an old shoebox from the top shelf. Pulled out the vodka bottle. Thank God. She'd never needed a drink more. *Leave her, would he? She'd show him.* She put the bottle to her lips and drank. A little "absolute'"courage. It hit her stomach with a warm silk thunderbolt, spread out to her arms and legs. She sank to the floor and tilted the bottle again. She didn't have to worry now, about walking that fine line, keeping her sober face on. She could lock herself up and drink to oblivion. Her husband had just walked out on her. Who wouldn't need a drink?

Lauren B. Davis

A Man Like That

"My mother should be glad she's got a man like that."

"No argument. I agree, your mother sure can be a pain in the butt," said Paula's boyfriend Calvin, "but you have to know how to handle her. She just wants someone to listen to her."

"I've been listening to her for years," said Paula, as she brushed her hair, "we've all been listening to her for years. I'm telling you, Daddy's been a saint. I don't know how he does it. Well, maybe I do. He seems to be able to just tune her out. I wish I could." She turned to face him. "OK, what do you think? It doesn't look too trashy?"

Paula wore a pale blue dress with a low-cut neck and no sleeves. Her feet were in strappy white high heels. It was too hot to let her hair hang down her back, so she'd put it up in a messy pile on the top of her head. She had gold hoops in her ears.

Calvin gave a low whistle and shook his hands as though the tips of his fingers were getting burned from just being this close to her.

"You trying to get me into some kinda fight tonight?" he teased.

"Well, you always did go for the trashy girls." She stuck out her tongue at him, crossed the small tidy room and picked up her straw bag from the bed. "Let's go. But please, Calvin, help me with Mum will you? She behaves better around you. It's only family she punishes."

It was a sticky hot Montreal evening in August. Paula's parents were visiting from Florida, as they did once every year. They were staying at the Queen Elizabeth Hotel, the last bastion of the English-speaking middle class. A few years ago Mr. and Mrs. Carson had retired to "The Sea Breeze", an adult inland community, where no breeze from the sea could ever be felt.

Mrs. Carson had warmed to the way of life in the land of sunshine and snowbirds. She enjoyed the group of ladies her own age, dances at the community centre, oranges and palm trees and no snow to shovel. They didn't know how long they'd be able to stay, though. Paula's mother was concerned that Mr. Carson's lack of financial acumen (and finances) meant they might be forced to come back. They couldn't afford American health insurance, an expensive necessity for people in what they referred to as the "golden years". She didn't want to come back to the bleak winters and was not pleased with Paula's father. He should have taken better care of their finances.

When he opened their hotel room door, Mr. Carson gave out a low whistle at the sight of his daughter.

"Well, well!" he said.

"Oh Daddy, stop it!" Paula laughed, and slapped him lightly on the arm.

"Hello, dear!" called out Mrs. Carson. Paula could see her coming out of the bathroom, wearing a dress covered in gigantic orange and blue flowers that she had doubtless made herself. "Hello there, Calvin! Give us a kiss! Don't you both look nice. Isn't this heat dreadful? I can't believe I'm still not used to it, even after living in Florida all this time. But of course there you can always go for a dip in the pool. Never mind, I've taken a couple of aspirin and my headache should go away. You know, I wanted to stay at the Sheraton. They have a pool there, but your father said it was too expensive. But really, he doesn't like the water, so we all have to suffer. Now if there was a hotel with a golf course, we'd be there in a jiffy, irregardless of the cost."

"'Regardless', Mother," said Paula.

"What?" she said.

"Paula was telling you the word is 'regardless', not 'irregardless', Sylvia", said Mr. Carson.

"Oh, for heaven's sake, who cares?" said Mrs. Carson.

"I'm with you, Mrs. C," said Calvin, who began herding the small group to the elevator.

The four of them walked through the lobby of the Queen Elizabeth Hotel. Paula walked with her father, while her mother and Calvin were a few steps behind. They passed the Algonquin Room Bar, a famous watering hole where Mr. Carson, who now went to AA meetings nearly every night, had no doubt done quite a bit of damage in his day. The hotel was very close to the office building where Mr. Carson had been vice-president in charge of pensions for a major life insurance company.

They were on their way to La Grill, the restaurant he had picked out, this being his old stomping grounds. It was a good restaurant, not too expensive, but the steaks were more than decent and the decor subdued.

As they walked across the lobby of the hotel, Paula slipped her arm through her father's arm. They had always been two peas in a pod, almost able to read each other's minds. She knew how exhausted he must be, locked up in that hotel room with her mother for hours, with nowhere to go to avoid her nagging. The way that woman picked on him was unforgivable.

Paula pulled herself close to her father, gave his arm a little squeeze and immediately felt him stiffen. It happened quick as a flash, so fast for a second she thought she'd misunderstood him, but she hadn't.

"Don't do that!" he said, and pulled himself away from her.

"Daddy?" Paula was baffled by the sudden turn.

Mr. Carson looked around, his eyebrows pulled down tight into a firm line. His lips pressed against each other so hard they were white around the edges. He scanned the crowd of people churning through the lobby. As clearly as if he'd said it out loud,

Paula sensed he was afraid he'd see someone he knew from his old firm, one of the men with whom he used to work. In that split second she saw his ferrety look around the room and knew, as she often knew what he was thinking, that he didn't want anyone with whom he was acquainted to see them, she with her arm wrapped through his, especially. And she knew why.

He was afraid they'd think he was with a woman best described as "not his wife". Which was something a man would only think of if at some point he had, in fact, walked through a hotel lobby with a woman not his wife.

Paula looked at her father, silently praying for a word or gesture that might now prove false the intuition she had always trusted. The possibility that she might have been so wrong about so much, and for so long, chilled her.

"Too damn hot for all that," Mr. Carson said, and he straightened his necktie, pulled down the cuffs of his shirt beneath his suit jacket and cleared his throat.

In the face of his flustered, uncharacteristic fidgeting, Paula felt as though someone had put a cold hand inside her stomach and then begun to squeeze.

Mr. Carson turned away from Paula, stepped back and joined his wife and Calvin, who were laughing together about something.

Paula stepped back and grabbed Calvin's arm.

"Ow! Hey, not so tight! You OK, babe?" he asked.

"Yes, I'm fine," she said, but she couldn't seem to take a deep enough breath.

"She's fine, just fine, aren't you, dear?" said Mr. Carson.

"Yes, Daddy," Paula said, not looking at him. She crossed her free arm over her breasts and kept walking straight ahead.

At the restaurant they automatically took their places at the round table, sitting as they always did. Mr. Carson sat between Paula and his wife. Calvin sat across from him. Mr. Carson suggested they all have steaks.

"They're damn good here, a high quality cut every time," he said.

"I think I'll have the swordfish," said Paula.

"Do you think you should dear, you don't really know how fresh fish is, do you?" said Mrs. Carson.

"It's what I want."

"Steak sounds good to me, Frank," said Calvin. "I like 'em rare."

Mr. Carson told the waiter they'd have three steaks, rare, not blue, but a good bloody red, and one swordfish, for the young lady.

The table was set very prettily with a small arrangement of tulips in the centre of the white cloth and twin sets of tiny brass salt and pepper shakers. Paula reached out and began to play with the salt and pepper shakers in front of her, setting them first close together and then far apart. Then she reached out and took the other salt shaker and formed a triangle. She pulled one away from the first set and placed it equidistant between the other two, noticing how nicely balanced it was.

"Paula, for God's sake, stop playing with those things," Mr. Carson said.

Mrs. Carson was saying something about the ballroom dancing lessons offered at the Sea Breeze Community Centre.

"...Yes, indeedy do! You should see some of these old codgers move! I've always wanted to take lessons, but of course Frank won't. Oh, he's promised to, but it's just like the shutters."

The issue of the shutters was a long-standing family joke. Each year Mr. Carson had promised to put shutters on the windows of their split-level house, and yet somehow never managed to get around to it. Each spring Mrs. Carson would ask, "Do you suppose this will be the year of the shutters?" And Mr. Carson would reply, "Oh, did you want shutters?" When they sold the house and moved south after living there for nearly twenty-three years, the windows were still shutter-free.

"What do you think, Paula? Should I find some other old coot to dance with me? I'll never get your father to go. You know your father!"

"Yeah, I know Dad. Better find somebody else, Mum." Paula smiled tightly at her mother.

"Hey, there! Don't start putting ideas in your Mum's head now!" laughed Calvin.

"I don't know, Calvin, nothing wrong with a few ideas, now is there? I think Mum's ideas are fine just the way they are."

Calvin half-smiled at Paula, although it was clear from the look on his face he didn't know if he was supposed to smile or not.

"Well, thank you dear!" laughed Mrs. Carson. "Although, of course, I'm not smart like you are. I've always said, even when you were a little girl, just how smart you were. Smart as a whip that one! You know Calvin, all her teachers said so..."

While Mrs. Carson chattered on like a happy sparrow, Paula and her father locked eyes across the table. It was Mr. Carson who broke away first. He looked down at the food in front of him and cut into the bloody meat with such force the plate let out an ear-splitting screech.

Smoke And Ash

And I've seen some hot, hot blazes/Come down
to smoke and ash...
   - *Joni Mitchell*

Winnie did not feel her best this Saturday morning. She'd been out late last night, cranking up the
volume with two girl friends, with peach schnapps,
with too many cigarettes. She hadn't had a black out,
more like a grey out. She remembered in which bars
they'd been, how she'd gotten home by cab. She
recalled wisely taking two aspirin and a couple of
vitamin C tablets before stumbling, still fully made
up and in her underwear, to bed. The particulars of
the night's conversation, however, were lost in a
bubble of aqueous fog. The phone numbers in her
purse were orphans. She had no idea to whom they
belonged, or if she'd made any accompanying ar-
rangements.

It didn't matter if she had though, for any ar-
rangements previously made were unimportant. The
phone rang at 10:30, jolting her poor head and stomach. It was Greg and he wanted to meet her at John's
Café at 12:30. She tried to sound as though she was

in the midst of something fascinating, instead of lying in bed trying not to puke. She didn't want him to know how wretched she felt, how hot and sticky and puffy and jangled. She normally wouldn't drink when she got up, well, rarely, but today was different. A drink would be curative. Necessary. To see Greg this unsteady, this vulnerable, was unthinkable.

She tossed a shot of brandy in her coffee to take the edge off. Purely medicinal. After two more such coffees, a couple of oranges and some toast, Winnie was in control again. Stomach only nominally churning, head clearing. She applied cold compresses to her face, tea bags to her eyes, took a long shower, perfumed and powdered. She was all right. The centre would hold.

It was a hot day. Sticky sidewalk hot. Melting dogs hot. Hot enough so that the diesel fumes from the trucks and gypsy cabs made stomachs queasy and heads ache. Winnie wore a thin slip of a dress, to show off her high breasts and good legs, under the pretence of keeping cool. She should have put her hair up, it was sticking to the back of her neck, but he liked her hair down. Her feet were gummy and starting to blister in the strappy high heels. She rolled the sweating cold glass of white wine along her throat. It felt good, and a couple of water drops eased their way down her cleavage, which wasn't a bad overall effect.

She'd made sure she'd arrived at the restaurant before Greg. Normally she would have made him wait for her, but today she wanted him to get the full effect of how she looked, sitting in the shade of the elm tree in the tiny garden terrace of John's Café. She composed herself to look assured and confidant, Hemingway's *A Moveable Feast* in front of her, a glass of wine in her hand, a languid air, slightly distant and desirable. A woman any man would want.

They'd been seeing each other regularly for the past two months. She was his girlfriend. She knew he thought of her that way. They loved each other, even if he hadn't come right out and said so. She had, of course, but women were always easier with words than men. His lack of reciprocal verbal devotion didn't mean a thing.

"I love you," she'd say, her ear against his slowing heartbeat.

"Winnie,..." She'd look at his wolfish face, expecting smiles, but his eyebrows were bunched up and his mouth thin.

He'd take a breath, readying himself to launch into words she didn't want to hear. She'd lay a finger on his lips.

"It's OK," she'd say. "It's OK."

She could wait. It would happen. He would say it.

She hadn't seen him since last Friday, the day before Cindy's wedding, at which she'd been the maid of honour. He'd promised to be there, but he'd stood her up. Furious, she'd called him from the reception and he'd made an excuse about some guys who'd shown up unexpectedly. Business he had to take care of. The editing business was like that. The film couldn't wait. She'd offered to come over in a couple of hours but he'd said it wasn't the place for her right now.

He'd sent flowers to her office the next day, as though that would make up for it. And, well,...it had. She was so happy to hear from him she giggled like an idiot all the way back to her desk, clutching the jolly daffodils and fragile mauve tulips. She was warmed by the idea that he was contrite, realising how wrong he'd been, begging her forgiveness. She knew she shouldn't let him off the hook just like that, but she wanted to, she wanted to so badly.

She wasn't fooling herself. He did care for her. She was convinced. The flowers were more than a polite gesture.

Winnie rolled the wine glass over her neck, tried to concentrate on Hemingway. She glanced at her watch. He was late. Her stomach rippled with nerves. She took a large swallow of the Chablis. She wanted to pull out her compact and make sure she wasn't all shiny, but she didn't want Greg to arrive and find her preening. She took a napkin and gently dabbed at her nose and chin, being careful not to smudge her powder.

The taxi arrived at last and the driver, a huge man with red blotches all over his face from the heat, and a roll of fat on his neck, heaved himself out and opened the trunk to get Greg's chair. It took Greg a moment to lock the wheel bolts, hop out of the back seat and get settled, snapping the foot rests into place and adjusting the pouch hanging off the back. Greg paid the driver and said something to him, then they both looked in Winnie's direction and the fat man laughed and high-fived Greg. Winnie smiled, took it as a compliment.

Greg rolled himself along the street a few feet to where there was a slope and he could get up the curb onto the sidewalk. He looked delicious, wearing a sparkling white sleeveless T-shirt that showed off his heavily muscled arms and shoulders to good advantage. The dragon tattoo on his left shoulder glinted with heat slick, making the blues and greens and yellows shine. Winnie imagined licking the sleek beast. His hair was black as sealskin, and his cheekbones stood out high and strong above the tidy goatee bracketing his soft mouth. She could feel the sweet gentle clench deep in her belly.

Greg rolled over to the white gate of the terrace and manoeuvred his way through the small metal tables to where she sat. He leaned forward and gave her a kiss, a quick one.

"Hey, babe, how's it going? You been waiting long?"

"No, not long," she brushed the back of her fingers against his face. "I missed you. You all right?"

"Yeah, I'm fine. Hot as hell. "

The waiter came over.

"Get me a Labatt's, OK? And another glass of wine for the lady."

Winnie was about to protest, she was on her second glass already, but then thought what the hell, why not? Being with Greg was a cause to celebrate in itself.

"Listen, I'm really sorry about the wedding."

She smiled and reached to take his hand, leaning over so the top of her dress gaped open just a little. "All is forgiven. The flowers were beautiful, it was a nice gesture."

"Weddings just aren't my thing," he said. "Too much coupledom, if you know what I mean."

Greg looked down at her hand holding his hand. He pulled his hand away and looked as though he was about to say something.

"I don't know. I like weddings. All that hope and belief in the future."

"Exactly," he said.

He rolled his top lip between his teeth and looked past her at the approaching waiter.

"Ah, great, the beer. Man, I cannot take this heat. " He wiped the back of his neck with a napkin and then lifted himself up off his chair a few inches, pushing up on the armrests with his hands.

The waiter put the drinks on the table and took away Winnie's already empty glass. Greg ignored his glass and tipped the bottle directly to his lips, taking a long hard pull at the cold beer. Winnie watched his Adam's apple move up and down and wanted to lean over and softly bite it.

Something was wrong with Greg. Normally, he leaned into her, running his fingers along her collarbone, down the inside of her arm. She knew he enjoyed displays of affection, as though proving his potential for sexuality to a disbelieving public. He liked to get people speculating about what he was capable of and what he was not.

They had met in a bar where Winnie had gone to see musician friends play. A bit of a dive, with cigarette butts on the floor and a bathroom with holes in the walls of the stalls, stuffed with toilet paper. Winnie had been the aggressor. She loved the way Greg looked, and, if the truth be known, the wheelchair had been part of the attraction. It wasn't simply the chair, she wasn't a freak, interested in cripples. It was the effect of him in the chair. If he had been a guy in a three-piece suit, it wouldn't have held any appeal, but because he looked like an outlaw biker, it added to his mystique. He looked tough. He looked dangerous. Tragedy enhanced him. What kind of a life must he have lived to end up broken like this? A terrible motorcycle accident? A gunshot? Some wild sports stunt? It was intriguing. And he was beautiful.

When Winnie walked, she glided. She knew this because she'd spent months as a teenager perfecting the way she moved. Her walk had often been called slinky by admiring men. She knew Greg noticed. Of course he noticed the way she moved.

Lauren B. Davis

What man would be more appreciative of her swaying undulations than a man who couldn't walk? It was perfect. By the end of the night she'd given him her phone number and he'd called her the next day.

They'd spent that weekend together, with Winnie learning many ways to please him. He'd been an excellent and uninhibited teacher. After they had explored each other in the tentative and exciting way of new lovers, he lay beside her and listened to her talk about all the things that mattered to her. He didn't fall asleep. He didn't sound bored, but asked her questions about why she'd left home so young, why she didn't see her family anymore. She'd found herself telling him about the bad things. Her father's disappearance when she was nine. Her mother's breakdown. And the good, like how she wanted to own a bookstore one day, with a café in the back, where people would come to talk about books, about life, about their dreams. She felt safe with Greg and thought they could be good for each other. She said so.

"It's all good," he said, and poured her another glass of brandy.

He told her about Linda, his ex, who left him after three years.

"Girl sure could pack a punch," he said.

"She *hit* you?"

"Damn right. Knocked me right off the fucking chair and then left me on the floor like a turtle on its back," he laughed. "Not that I don't admit I deserved it."

"What on earth could you have done?"

"Let's just say she caught me with my fingers in a pie other than hers."

"Oh."

"Hey, don't look like that. I learned my lesson. One girl at a time for me. That's the way to keep things friendly."

She didn't like the sound of the word "friendly", but it was early days yet.

It was fine, the first few weeks, fine enough to keep her waiting by the phone, ready to go over and see him whenever he called. But he was secretive. Kept his distance. Just typical male fear of commitment, she was sure. She wanted more. She wanted him to ask her to live with him. She wanted to be part of his world, firmly and incontrovertibly.

"What have you been up to this week? I didn't hear from you."

"You shouldn't hang around waiting for me. You should go out, do things."

"I'm not hanging around, for God's sake. I went out last night as a matter of fact. Had a blast. I do have a life, you know," Winnie laughed, making light of his criticism. "What about you?"

"I had some things I had to do. You know how it is. Things get busy. So, you had a good time?"

"Yeah, we had a great time. We went to a few clubs, danced all night. I don't think I got back until about 4:00 this morning."

"That's great." He nodded his head and beamed at her as though she'd achieved some major personal breakthrough.

"But," Winnie reached over and took his hand in hers, "I would have had a better time if you'd been there. I don't get to see enough of you these days."

"Yeah, well...," he frowned, took a deep breath and leaned forward, "that's sort of what I wanted to talk to you about."

Oh shit. He's dumping me. She pulled back her hand. She took a drink of her wine. She looked at him. She composed her face into the slight smile she knew showed off her cheekbones to best advantage.

"Really?"

"Listen Winnie, you know I told you when I first met you that I'd just ended a three-year relationship with somebody. And I'm not ready to get re-involved again just now. What I'm looking for is a friend really, just someone to hang out with now and then."

I don't believe this. He's dumping me? After he stood me up? You should pardon the pun.

"You know, you're really an amazing woman. It's just bad timing is all. I've got some stuff happening in my life these days and I need to not be tied up in a relationship. I mean, you can see, like about the wedding, I'm not in a space where I can be real dependable."

"I didn't make a big deal about the wedding. I don't know what makes you think I want some big involved relationship..."

"Yeah, you're probably right. I'm probably way off track here. I'm gonna have another beer - you want another glass of wine, or something else maybe? You want a margarita?"

Usually he didn't encourage her to drink. In fact, the opposite was closer to the truth.

"Hey, aren't you the guy always lecturing me about my alcohol consumption?"

He'd done more than that, actually. He'd disappeared on her the last time they went dancing at The Warehouse. She'd just downed a couple of tequila shots with Andy, the blonde muscle god-bartender with the gold ring in his lip, when Greg announced he was leaving.

"Winnie," he said, pulling on her dress to get her attention, "I'm outta here."

"What do you mean? It's not late."

"I've had enough. Looks like you have, too."

"Every party needs a pooper," said Andy, blowing a kiss at Greg.

"Don't go. Stay. Dance with me!" She leaned on the arms of his chair and pushed him backward toward the dance floor. Somebody must have spilled a drink, because her high-heeled foot slid out from under her and, unbalanced as she was, she landed on her knees, with her head in Greg's lap.

"That's one way to get him to stay, Sweetheart!" yelled Andy over the bass thrum. "How about me next?"

"Winnie, get up! Are you all right?" Greg helped her to her feet. She couldn't stop laughing.

"Why don't you come with me?" he said.

"Oh, come on!" she said, between hiccups of giggles. "Don't be so *boring*!" She closed her eyes and swung her hips in a belly-dance swirl designed to mesmerise.

When she opened her eyes he was gone.

But now he was saying: "So do you want another drink or not?"

"Whatever," she said.

"Waiter, can I have another beer and a margarita? "

"Do you know what you're doing? I mean do you really know?" Winnie looked directly in his eyes, those beautiful dark eyes. She shouldn't be saying this, what was the point? The best course of action would be to smile gently and say no to another drink. The best course of action would be to leave, dignity intact.

"Do you know what you're turning down?" she said.

"I'm probably making a big mistake, a mistake I'll really regret."

"You probably will. Excuse me a minute..."

Winnie walked, fairly steadily she thought, to the bathroom and looked in the mirror. She looked OK, a little pale, but OK. She went into the stall and used the toilet, came out and washed her hands in cold water, patting them dry along the inside of her arms and the back of her neck. She reapplied her lipstick. She fluffed her hair. She had no intention of crying. None at all. It was absurd.

If she handled this right, she'd keep him. He was gun-shy after his long involvement with Linda of the mean left hook. All men were afraid of commitment, weren't they?

When they'd first come together he said he'd been drawn to her because she was so together, so independent. She could be those things again. She would be the cool, calm woman, with no tears, no pleading, no hysterics. He would see her icy desirability and long for her again. Her mistake had been to be too open, too vulnerable in her love for him. It was a tactical error she could remedy.

She didn't want to lose him. *How on earth would she explain to her friends she'd been dumped by Greg, of all people?* She shook her head. Mustn't give in to anger. Mustn't lose her cool.

She returned to the table, wishing Greg wasn't watching her walk; it made her self-conscious and awkward. The new drinks were on the table. She sipped the sour concoction. It tasted good.

Lauren B. Davis

She felt finely tuned, not tight, but taut. She needed to hit just the right note. She ran her fingers up and down the side of the glass. They said nothing for a few minutes.

Just to keep the buzz on the right level, she kept taking sips of her drink. She vowed not to be the first to speak.

"I love you," she said, angling her head so that the dappled light through the trees made her eyes bright.

"I care about you, too."

"You don't get that many chances in your life to have someone love you."

"I know that. I just need to be uninvolved romantically right now."

He's in a wheelchair, for Christ's sake; doesn't it occur to him he should be happy to have me? She wasn't proud of the thought, but it was true wasn't it?

"I see." She couldn't seem to let well enough alone. She knew he probably wanted nothing more than to get out of here intact, without a big scene. It was classic, him choosing the restaurant as his good-bye venue. Classic. "I'm not prone to making scenes. You didn't need to stage this."

"I didn't think of it that way. I just wanted to see you in person."

"You mean you considered dumping me over the phone?"

"No, of course not, I'm not *dumping* you... I only want to be clear, you know, about where things are going."

"Apparently they're going nowhere... Well? That's what you mean isn't it?"

"I guess so. Look, I'm sorry," Greg said. He looked around, embarrassed. *Was her voice too loud? Where did that drink go?* Her head was spinning.

"Then I don't suppose there's much more to say. I'd better be going. I've got lots to do this afternoon." Her lips felt thick. "Many things to do."

She tried to take another drink but the straw's slurping sound told her it was futile.

She looked over her glass, found Greg looking back at her. He looked worried.

140

"Do you know what you're giving up? I want you to know what you're giving up." She was starting to cry. Her words were slurry.

"Look, I'll call you a cab, OK? You're in no condition to take a bus back."

She shook the empty margarita glass at him.

"Answer me! Do you know? Do you?"

Greg didn't answer her. He looked at the empty glass in her hand. It was clear. He knew. She could see he knew.

Lauren B. Davis

Celestial Bodies

"I am afraid," said Celeste.

"Of what," said Philippe.

"Of you. That you will break me."

"Well, I might," he said, laughing. "Will you stay anyway?"

Celeste did not answer, but neither did she leave. She turned to look through the slats of the wooden shutters to the shadows passing in the late afternoon sun.

It was very warm in the room. A sheen of perspiration lay on their skin and puddled in the hollow of her stomach, where so recently his tongue had left a wetness of its own.

He reached over and lifted a whisper of tobacco-coloured hair from her eyes. He had clay beneath his fingertips and spatters of paint on the pants he had not bothered to fully remove. She lay on lavender-washed silk. There were plum circles beneath her eyes.

It had only been a week since his work had been received with such great success.

Six months before, he met her at the market. He startled her, running up to her as she picked through cabbages and potatoes. He was a large man, over six feet, with the body of an athlete. His hair curled below his ears and was grey at the temples. His mouth full, the lips red as berries, the teeth white and strong. His eyes were the colour of rain.

"Didier, look at her, look at this one!" he exclaimed loudly to his companion, a little man with a soft face and round glasses.

"Yes, yes, lovely," said that one.

He danced around her, plucking at her clothes, her hair.

"Monsieur! What do you think you are doing?" she swiped at his hands.

"The voice of an angel! I knew it would be so! And grace, she is like a dancer. Tell me, Celestial One, are you a dancer?"

"What I am is of no concern to you, except that I am a stranger, and wish to remain so! Leave me alone! I will call the gendarmes!"

"So, you do not know who I am?"

"I do not care who you are!"

"Brava! Quick, Didier, introduce me before she bolts."

"Mademoiselle, may I have the honour of introducing you to Philippe Pitton, the greatest artist in Paris."

"Didier! Only in Paris? You're fired!"

"Did I say Paris? Of course, I meant in the world!"

"You are re-hired!" He turned to Celeste and bowed low, removed his hat and swept the filthy market floor with it. "At your service!"

Celeste was taken aback. Philippe Pitton! Who had not heard of Pitton?

"My dear, may I present you,..." the little man waited to hear her name.

"Celeste Cabriot," she found herself saying.

"Celeste! Celeste! Didier, did I not say it? An angelic spirit. It is fate I tell you, fate!" Philippe took her hand. "My angel, you are the answer to my prayers."

Three weeks later she moved into his apartment.

He was a force she could not resist. He enveloped and exposed her. There was not an inch of her body he did not explore. The inside of her arm, with its twin moles, the place where her buttocks folded to the leg, the hollow of her armpit, the spot behind her ear, the arch of her foot. She was electric wherever he touched her. She began to believe everything that had come before him was mere illusion.

She knew she had usurped someone. He did not hide the evidence. A slipper by a chair. A stocking fallen like foam beside the bed. A pot of face cream. The smell of perfume in the wardrobe. When she questioned him he said only that the woman was no longer a part of him.

"Why do you want to know this? What has it to do with you?"

"I am only curious, Philippe, it is natural to want to know something of your life, of your loves before me."

"HA! There have been a thousand before you! Does that please you? You are morbid. The woman became a horror. You need know nothing more." He took her face in his hands, held her there. "Concentrate on this, now, here. You are my art now, and my art is my life. It is enough."

Celeste hardly noticed that as she abandoned herself to him, he became cruel to her. She was not permitted to speak when he painted her, or when he used his hands roughly on his small mounds of clay, pinching and pressuring them to his will. He now spent long periods of time examining her intently, commenting on imperfections, an awkward proportion, a mole, a fleshy curve of which he did not approve. She twisted to turn away from his magnifying gaze, the burning it left on her skin.

"You must not be afraid of the truth," he said, forcing her to be still. "Truth is where art resides."

He formed thin, reed-like figures from his impressions of her, elongated and fragile, from clay, from copper. He drew her as a crane, as an eel in the beak of a crane. He painted her as a wraith.

Lauren B. Davis

Her friends wanted to know why she stayed with him. They
knew his reputation. All Paris knew his reputation. Sometimes in
the evenings Philippe banished her, saying he must be alone to
work, without her breathing, her beating heart, distracting him.
She went to La Gentilhommiere on rue St. André des Arts. There,
Sylvie and Jean-Paul badgered her.

"He is a beast. You are not the first," said Sylvie, who drank
absinthe like a potion.

"He is old, too old for you. He knows too much about
women, and what he knows he hates," said Jean-Paul. "You will
never be able to protect yourself."

"But I don't want to protect myself," said Celeste.

"Then you are a fool," said Jean-Paul. "Have you not seen
his wife? She wanders the streets, a huge toad, looking for his
work in the galleries and when she finds it... Oh, la! Such a
scene! She broke a window, I heard, in the 7th. She is a monster,
and she is his creation!" His fist hit the table and the glasses
rattled.

"What has she to do with me?"

"She is still obsessed with him," said Sylvie. "All the others
are. After him, they say, no one else will do. They become bloated
with their need for him."

"I am not them."

"Wait. He will infect you. Grow in you like a tumour. Always it begins the same, with some willow-girl, and then - pah!
He is evil as opium."

"What do you know? I know! I am so alive when I am with
him! He is something new in the world, an artist with a vision
never seen before. Even in New York, in Rome, they clamour for
him."

"Celeste, I have known you for years. Since school. Look at
me," said Sylvie. "I know he makes you cry. You must see it is his
pleasure to do so. Admit it."

"I will admit no such thing. You don't understand."

"I understand this: where other parasites suck the blood from
their victims, he ejaculates poison into his."

"Don't be disgusting," said Celeste. She wrapped her wool-

146

len scarf around her neck and stormed out.

The name of his new show was *Celestial Bodies*, and was a great success. The critics praised him. He sold many works.

"Look at the delicacy," people said.

"Look at the ethereal quality."

All the figures so delicate, like trees in a quiet forest, leaf bare, reduced to the bones of birds. All the shades of paint like cirrus vapour, like prayer.

His arm around her, he exhibited her also. He lifted her arm to show the pose in front of a statue. In front of a painting he turned her to reveal the sweep of bones in her spine through the thin material of her dress.

"It is all due to your perfection, my angel." He buried his face in her neck and she glowed.

Quickly, however, the glow turned to chill.

For three months after his success, he could not work. He drank. He ranted. He turned away from her, frequented whores and came home smelling of them, of ashes and herring.

"You are fat," he said one morning.

The morsel of croissant in her mouth turned to plaster.

"I am not."

"Yes, look at yourself. You are dough!" He reached over and grabbed her belly, hurting her, twisting the flesh.

She began to cry and slapped away his hand.

"You don't love me anymore!" she sobbed. "You are heartless!"

"Women!" he bellowed. "You are all the same! You do not last!"

"Have you no pity? You are my life!"

"And art is mine! If you want me, you too, must be art!"

She ran sobbing from the room.

One day they went to the Jardin du Luxembourg, because he said he wanted to get very drunk at the café near the Medici fountain.

"This will greatly annoy the waiter," he said, pleased at the prospect, for in his present state he sought only to create the most violent emotions possible.

As they entered the gates they saw a crowd of people and he went toward them, eager as always for new stimuli, new experiences.

A group of circus performers celebrated the birthday of the lady snake charmer. They were like a medieval troupe of jugglers and acrobats, dressed in colourful clothes, advertising their playful life. They passed bottles of wine, bowls of olives, piquant sausages, figs and bread. Their children were feral as cats. A young man wearing a hat from which hung silver bells played guitar and sang suggestive songs. The trapeze artists danced with each other.

Philippe joined the group. He drank wine. He was like Bacchus among the revellers. The tightrope walker, who wore many bangles on her arms and gold hoops in her ears, like a gypsy, and the lion tamer, with his fine muscles and deep scars, sat near him. He told them they were all painters and sculptors, only their medium was different. Where he used pigment and clay, they used their bodies and the air itself.

Celeste sat beneath a tree and watched him. She was aware of the lithe and limber bodies all around her. The waistband of her skirt felt too tight, and this a new skirt, bought when the old one would no longer fit.

"You are perhaps the greater artists," he flattered them, "for your very appearances are evidence of your talent. Your bodies are your canvases, your blocks of granite."

"Laing-Laing," the lion tamer called, "come here and show this man what you can do! A miracle, Monsieur, you will not believe."

From the group stepped an exquisite creature, delicate as spun glass. Her long black hair was tied in a swatch thick as a horse's tail. She wore shimmering silver Chinese pyjamas.

"A contortionist from the Orient," the lion tamer whispered in Philippe's ear. "Watch her."

The girl pranced towards Philippe.

She raised her hands above her head and bent her body like

a bow, backwards, until her forehead touched the ground. Her sex was now the highest point, atop her open legs. She curled herself still more, until her face appeared between her sharp ankles and she rested on her forearms. She lifted her feet and rested them on her shoulders. She was a body inverted on itself, the perspective altered, so that she was sex first and all else second. Her face was placid, serene, porcelain.

From under the shade of the tree, Celeste never took her eyes from Philippe. He was sweating. His eyes were no longer like rain. They were like lightening. She turned and ran from the park.

He came home very late that night. Very drunk. He crashed and hurled himself up the stairs. He threw open the door and found Celeste standing naked in front of a mirror, where she had stood, immobile, for hours. Her buttocks were heavy. Her waist thick. Seen from the back there was a lump of fat on either side of her body, a plump of flesh just above the hip. Her thighs flattened themselves against each other. On her legs were bloody spider webs of tiny veins. There was a fold in her belly. Her breasts drooped.

Philippe wove towards her.

"So, you see it now yourself," he slurred. He slapped her breasts from side to side while she stood, pliant as mud. Picked up first one and then the other, weighing. "Overripe. Bulbous..." he muttered.

He turned from her and fell across the bed, where he began to snore loudly and wetly.

Celeste moved to the long table where Philippe kept his tools. She chose a very sharp knife, weighing it in her hand as he had weighed her flesh. She turned back to the mirror. She took a handful of her flesh, just there, below the belly button and above the pubic hair. She pulled it as far away from her body as she could. She lowered the knife to the skin, feeling how cold it was. She looked at her reflection, imagining the work of art she would create from this flesh, the lines, the contours, the shadows, the rich, deep colours.

She felt the warmth of her body's muscle and sinew and bone under the yielding, elastic tissue. Felt a trickle of sweat beneath her arm. Celeste turned and looked at Philippe, mouth open, hair sticking to his forehead, the buttons of his pants undone.

Celeste turned from the mirror and approached the bed, the knife still in her hand.

She thought: I will do what he has done, I will make art from the lives of others.

Yours Truly

You walk out the door and down the stairs, with your suitcase banging on the wooden steps and his voice clanging in your head. You start down the road, one hand on the opening of your coat, which you didn't have time to button. It hurts where the wool touches the inside of your arm, but you aren't going to let that stop you. Just to be gone. That's the one thought in your head.

Better move fast. He'll probably be out for hours, but you never know.

The cold air feels good on your heated-up face. Everything has that squished-worm smell it gets after a hard rain. You watch where you walk. Ordinarily you pick up any stranded ones and put them, wriggling with gratitude, into some soft piece of earth. But you don't have time for that tonight.

You figure maybe you'll go to Gary's place and maybe he'll let you stay and maybe he won't because Diane doesn't like you. Either way, Gary will at least let you in 'cause he knew this was coming. You think he'd probably do more than just lend a helping hand, except he's married and you know he's married and you don't go in for that kind of stuff, even if his wife doesn't believe that for a minute.

"That girl hangs around here too much," you heard her say the last time you were over and down sweeping up the cobwebs and mouse turds.

"I told her I'd pay her a couple of bucks to clean up the basement," Gary said, his voice low.

"I don't like it. I don't want her around here no more."

"Give her a break, Di, she needs the money. She's just a kid."

"Kid my ass. She's old enough," Diane said, so you could hear it loud and clear.

Diane's just jealous 'cause she's not seventeen anymore and won't be again. It's not your fault her husband likes to look at you and talk to you. You like talking to him but you'd never do anything else. What makes her think you'd even be interested in old Gary with his sofa butt and beer belly?

No, Diane probably won't let Gary let you stay. But you can use the phone. You think you'll stay at the Belvedere Hotel. It's the only hotel in town that's not a motel and the motel isn't real safe, with the plywood doors and rowdy bikers coming and going. The Belvedere Hotel has a reception area beside the lunch counter and nobody's supposed to be able to get upstairs unless you go through old starch-haired Mrs. Lyons first.

Staying there would be the right way to start off your new life. You could have a bath and watch TV and maybe order up a hamburger. They'd bring it to you on a tray, with a bucket of ice and a folded napkin, right to your door and you'd tip the kid who brought it.

As you walk up Prince Street this guy pulls up in a Lincoln Town Car and sticks his head out the window. He's got a slicked-down comb-over and broken blood vessels on his cheeks. He's got a cigar between his thick fingers and you catch the cheap nose-burning smell even from where you are.

"Hey, you need a lift?" he says.

And you say,

"No, thank you," real polite but firm to let him know you're not a little piece of chicken just waiting for him to carve a slice.

"I'm going all the way to Halifax," he says, like that's the only destination in the whole world. He drives slow alongside you.

"Have a nice drive," you say, hoping it sounds like icicles falling on the sidewalk.

A lady comes up the street with a wheezy Pekinese on a pink leash and she looks at you and this guy and he sees her and takes off. You just know he's got a wife and kids and a stubby hard-on under his polyesters. The lady passes you and gives you a wide berth like she doesn't want to get dirty touching you. You were going to be polite and say "Good evening" and maybe you were hoping she'd talk to you for a minute. But now you're just pissed at yourself for thinking that and you don't say anything to her either.

You keep your eyes straight ahead and change your suitcase to the other hand because it's getting heavy and the plastic handle cuts into your palm. The weight of it pulls your arm close to your body and the material rubs against the part that hurts. It's so bad you almost cry out but you don't. You just change hands back again.

You stop for a minute on Gary's doorstep, pat down the rain frizz in your hair and wipe away any mascara streaks. You hope it's Gary who answers the door and not Diane. You go to ring the bell, but there's a wire sticking out and you don't like the look of it, so you bang on the door. Nobody comes and you can hear Bruce Springsteen singing away about America, so you bang again, hard enough to hurt your knuckles.

"Jesus, what're you doing here?" says Diane, with a cigarette between her lips and a sweatshirt on that says, "Baby on Board", even though there isn't any baby.

"Think I can come in? Just for a minute," you say, and you're afraid you're going to start to cry.

"Gary!" she calls out. "You better come deal with this."

"What's up?" he says, then sees you at the door. "Chrissie, what happened? Are you OK?"

"More or less."

"You better come in," he says. He's got on old jeans with grease on them and no socks or shoes. You can see a swipe of his white belly between his T-shirt and his belt.

"Gary..." says Diane, with that flat sort of warning in her voice that means they've talked all this over before and he better stick to what he agreed.

"Chill out, Diane," he says. He looks at her sharp with his pale eyes and motions for you to come in. He's got a bandage on his hand.

"What'd you do?" you say.

"Wrench slipped. No big deal." Gary's always puttering around on that old Harley of his and he's always hurting himself one way or the other.

"Thanks," you say, as he takes your suitcase and puts it inside the door. Not too far, you notice.

"You want to tell me what's going on?" he says.

"Yes, Chrissie, why don't you do that?" says Diane, her hands folded across her skinny flat chest.

"Why don't you go watch Jerry Springer or something?" he says.

"No."

"Don't be a bitch. Just gimme a couple of minutes, OK?"

"Deal with this, Gary. I mean it," she says and flounces off down the hall.

"OK, kid," says Gary, standing with his hands tucked up under his armpits and his head cocked to one side. "Tell me. You in trouble?"

"I guess."

"You leave Dexter?"

"Yeah."

"It's about fucking time. He coming after you?" Gary looks out the little window in the top of the door, squinting his eyes through the smudgy glass.

"Not for a while anyway. He was passed out when I left. I don't figure he'll be doing much of anything till morning."

"Booze?"

"That's how he started."

"What else?"

"Smack. He's been going again since last week."

Gary whistled low. "Well, at least he'll be harmless for a few hours. He hurt you?"

"He always hurts me."

"This time?"

So you push up your sleeve and you show him. He winces and makes like he's going to touch them, but then doesn't. He puts his arm around your shoulder and you feel so brittle you could crinkle and pop into dust.

"Bastard. I could fucking kill him."

"He's doing a pretty good job of that himself," you say and fiddle with the little silver crucifix on your neck. The one Dex gave you instead of a wedding ring.

"What are you going to do?"

"Well, I guess I can't stay here, can I? Just for a night or two?"

"I wish I could say yes, kid. I really do. If it was just me, it wouldn't be a problem. But you know Diane. You know how it is."

"There's no reason."

"You know that, and I know that, but Diane's got baggage. Sorry." And he looks like he really means it, which is nice, but doesn't help.

"You need money?"

"No. I got a couple of hundred I been squirrelling away."

"That's not going to get you too far. Maybe you should go home."

"No fucking way," you say. "Not in a million years."

"It was just a suggestion." But he doesn't push it, because you've told him everything.

"So?"

"So, I gotta get lost."

"Yeah, I think that's best."

"I'll get a room for the night. Take off tomorrow. Can I use your phone?"

"Yeah. Sure. You know where it is."

So you go into Gary and Diane's kitchen which is deco- rated with these stupid geese everywhere with ribbons around their necks that Diane thinks is the height of style. It smells like the kitty litter should be changed.

"Belvedere," says the women's stuffy-nosed voice.

"I'd like to reserve a room for tonight, please."

"For *tonight?*"

"Yes." You should have gone straight there. It probably seems weird to want a room for the night when it's already past ten, but you know why you didn't. It's less humiliating to be turned down over the phone.

"I'm not sure anything's available," the voice says. Which you know is a huge pile of steaming shit because this is not a town where the hotel rooms ever get full. "May I have your name please."

"Mrs. Bowen," you say, because she's gonna know who you are when you show up anyway, but you think using the "Mrs." might make it harder to refuse you.

"Why do you need a hotel room?"

And you think, *What kind of a question is that?*

"I'd just like to rent a room. For one night." But you know it's no good, you know she knows who you are and she's not going to give you a room.

"I'm sorry, we seem to be full up. Maybe you'd better go home, Honey." And she hangs up. Bitch. Fucking small towns. Everybody knowing everything about everybody and making judgment even when you didn't do anything wrong and are doing your best to get the fuck away from the crap-fest that your life's turned into.

Gary comes into the kitchen holding a white plastic first aid kit.

"We should take a look at that arm."

"It's OK." You don't want him to know about the other places. "Can I take the kit with me?"

"Yeah. Sure. You get a room?"

"I'm going to over to the Indian Head."

"I wish you could stay here..."

"Don't sweat it. Dex'd come here anyway," you say, which makes you think. "Hey, what're you gonna do if he does shows up?" You feel bad. You don't want to bring that kinda trouble down on Gary. Even if he is twice Dex's size, when Dex gets crazy mean he's a whole truckload of dangerous.

"You don't worry about that kiddo. I kinda hope he does."

"Oh, fine! And what about me?" says Diane, who must have heard and is standing in the doorway with a beer dangling from one hand and the other hand on her bony hip. "I suppose I don't rate worrying about."

"Nothing's gonna happen to you, Di."

"You're right there, bud. None of that shit for this girl. I wouldn't have put up with that crap for half a minute. I'd been gone the first time it ever happened." She blows smoke right in your face.

What Diane doesn't know would fill up a football stadium.

"Can I give you a lift up to the Indian?" says Gary.

"Thanks," you say.

"I'm going too," says Diane, which you figured.

As she goes to get her coat, Gary slips you fifty bucks.

"It ain't much, but it's all I've got."

"I'll get it back to you."

"Just get yourself on your feet, someplace far away, OK?" he says and gives you that sweet smile of his that makes you not care that his teeth aren't so good.

You sit on the bed in the motel room, trying to ignore the crackle of the plastic sheet under the thin blanket. There's a rerun of *Rosanne* on the TV. The door to the bathroom has a poster of a kitten dangling by its tiny paws from a bar, its mouth wide open in terror. *Hang in there baby*, it says. When you go to the bathroom the poster swings out and shows the big hole somebody punched in the door.

You think about Dex sitting back at the apartment smoking a cigarette in the dark and blowing on the ember end until it gets bright red and hot enough to do the sick shit he wants it to do. He's going to wake up in the morning and think you're going to come crawling back for more 'cause how can a girl your age make it on her own.

You think about the note you left on the kitchen table next to a little pool of olive oil and drain cleaner with Dex's junk dissolving in it and four empty cellophane packs to let him know you'd found them all. You half hope he'll try and mainline it and do everybody a favour.

The note said it all.

Fuck you. Yours truly, Chrissie.

Tomorrow you'll get a bus to Halifax and find a job waitressing or something. You count out your money on the bed. Fives and ones and change and a ten or two, saved from grocery allowance and snitched from drug stash money when Dex wasn't looking. It's not much to show, considering what you had to do to earn it.

You try and get some sleep, because it's been one hell of a day and you worry about how long the cash will hold out. Maybe you should have taken that guy's offer of a lift after all. Maybe he'll be out there again tomorrow.

Sensitive Things

Alice tried to ignore it, but failed. She'd chipped a tooth, and every time she spoke her tongue rubbed against it. Like something was caught in there. Just the sort of thing that would turn out to be nothing at all, unless she didn't have it seen to, in which case it would be an abscess, a root canal, something impacted.

She didn't have a dentist in Newbury anymore. She'd been gone too many years. Twenty years. She only came back once a year to see her parents, keep up with old friends. Her dentist was thousands of miles away, back in London, which she now called home. She asked friends. *Do you have a good dentist? Someone you really trust? Will he hurt me?* Alice had a stomach-cramping fear of dentists.

She was at Cindy's house. Cindy of the long brown legs and French manicured hands and perfect Martha Stewart life. The two old friends stood in the kitchen drinking tall glasses of cold water and lemon from sweating glasses. After-tennis drinks for ladies over forty. Something to replenish the cells rather than make the mood merry.

"My dentist will see you. He's a darling."

159

"I don't want a darling. I want someone who won't stick a needle all the way up to my brain."

"Alice, you are a coward." Cindy was already dialling, using a pencil to poke the numbers on the phone so as not to ruin her nails.

"Yes. When it comes to dentists, I'm definitely a coward."

"Wait... Hello? Yes, oh, I'm so glad I caught you in. My oldest friend's here from London, Doctor, and she's done something dreadful to her tooth."

"It's not that dreadful," Alice said. "It's probably nothing."

"I realise you're not really working today, but I thought... as a special favour to me?"

"If he's busy, tell him it's not important... it can wait."

"Oh, I told her you were a darling! She'll be right over. Thanks. Bye."

"He'll see me?"

"He'll see you."

"Great."

"Don't be such a feeb! I'll drive you. We have to go right away. He was just in the office finishing up paper work and he's waiting. Come *on!*"

In the Range Rover, Alice checked her face in the mirror on the back of the sun visor. After two and a half hours of tennis, she looked pretty much as you'd expect. Sweaty, blotchy, dehydrated. Without make-up she looked every one of her forty years.

"My hair looks like seaweed on a rock. Why can't I have your hair?"

Cindy had masses of golden tresses cascading down her back.

"You can. Hair extensions. All you need is money and time, sweetums, and anyone can be ravishing."

"Really, even *me?*" Alice raised an eyebrow peered over the top of her sunglasses at Cindy.

"Don't be ridiculous, you're already ravishing. Besides you're going to see Dr. Falud, the dentist, not Carlo, the tennis pro - who, you must admit, is stunning."

"This guy's name is Falud?"

"Yes. Why?"

"Not Omar Falud?"

"God, you know him?"

"I hope not," she said and sank down into her seat.

"Tell me!"

"He must be what, late fifties now? Tall, thin-lipped, tons of black hair, used to be married to this wild New Yorker named Rita?"

"Age is right, lips are right, but the hair's all white now, and he's just gone through his third divorce, so I can't keep track. How do you know him?"

"He asked me to marry him once."

"You are kidding!"

"It was a long time ago. I was very young. I get the feeling he liked 'em young. Teachable. He gave me the impression of being a man who liked to be boss. And he had two kids already. He had custody. I couldn't see myself as a step-mother at nineteen. I turned him down." Alice looked out the window. "It was very odd. All very formal and old world. He never even kissed me. Just kept having me meet more and more of his family. He spoke to Daddy before he spoke to me."

"Your father must have been furious. He's loaded, I mean really loaded. All that money from Iran or Iraq or Saudi or wherever the hell he's from."

"He wasn't furious, for God's sake," she grinned, "but he did ask me if I was really, really, *really* sure."

Cindy laughed. "Well, here's your big chance. You're both between spouses at the moment."

"Maybe he won't remember me. It's been 21 years. He knew me as Alice Carter, not Alice Webster. He probably won't make the connection. And for your information, I am not between spouses. I'm divorced, once and for all. No more for me."

"I'll come in with you," said Cindy.

"The hell you will," said Alice. "Go buy a new Mercedes or something."

"Party pooper," said Cindy, and stuck her tongue out.

Lauren B. Davis

Dr. Falud's office was immaculate. A Persian carpet on the floor. Ivory walls with line drawings and charcoal sketches and tasteful watercolours. Pale rose leather couches. The receptionist's desk was empty, must be her day off. Alice waited alone for a moment, thinking he must have heard the discreet chime of the bell as she opened the door.

"Hello," she called out.

"Yes, yes, please come back," he answered.

She walked down the short corridor and saw him in his office. Leather chair, leather topped desk, more Persian antique carpets on the floor. Good paintings on the wall. A Modigliani, probably real.

"I'm Ms. Webster," she held out her hand. "It's so good of you to see me on your day off."

He stood and shook her hand.

He had aged, but then who hadn't? Where he used to have the body of a tango dancer, now there was a soft pot belly. His shoulders had shrunk. It looked as though his body had slipped, sliding down until it settled in a little pouchy roll around his middle. His hair was snow white, but his eyes, those dark desert eyes, were still as compelling as ever.

"I just came in to catch up on the paperwork. You must forgive me," he said indicating his clothes, "I am not dressed properly to see patients." He wore a beige cashmere sweater and black pants creased to a knife's edge. His voice still held the faint accent of his Arab mother tongue, the exotic, vaguely erotic lilt.

Alice was very aware of how she looked, sweat pants and T-shirt with stains under the arms, running shoes. She probably didn't smell very good.

"I'm not dressed for seeing a dentist," she joked. "Just came off the tennis courts." She remembered this formality in his speech, and the sense of being just a little improper, in need of his correcting influence.

"It is nothing," he said, with no trace of irony, unfortunately. "Tell me, what you have done? What has happened to your tooth?" He kept his eyes on her face. But there was no hint he knew who she was. Just very professional.

"Well, I doubt it's anything really. I was flossing, I do floss, you'll be happy to hear," she paused, but was rewarded with only the merest hint of a polite smile, "anyway, I think I may have taken a nick out of a filling or something. It feels like something's caught in there."

"You have a filling there, yes?"

"I think I do. I'm such a chicken when it comes to dentists I'm never conscious when they do the filling. Just knock me out, I say, let me have the Demerol and I'm a happy camper."

"What an interesting approach. Why don't we go into the examining room and I'll take a look. Please..." He indicated she should precede him across the hall into another room.

As she settled herself in the chair, noticing with some trepidation the nearby implements of potential torture, Dr. Falud washed his hands and put on his white coat behind a partition.

"Have we met before, Mrs. Webster? Your face is very familiar to me. Perhaps you have been a patient of mine in the past?"

"Well, I wasn't going to say anything. I was going to see if you remembered. My name used to be Carter. Alice Carter? I lived on Silcox Lane. We were acquainted once, a long time ago."

Dr. Falud returned. "Yes, of course. I remember you well. You are just as beautiful as you were," he smiled a flawless smile, "when, fifteen years ago?"

"A little longer, but I'll only admit to fifteen."

"I remember your delightful sense of humour. Why don't we take a look at that tooth? Open please."

She opened her mouth obediently. She felt vulnerable. Dentists' chairs, the reclining posture, all of it seemed vaguely sadomasochistic. She was aware of his nearness and the minty smell of his gloved hands. *Did medical gloves come in flavours now, like condoms?*

"Yes," he said, "you have a tiny filling there. Very small. Probably you have chipped a minute portion of it."

"Unghuh," she said.

Alice felt flushed, alone with him in the office, his face so

Lauren B. Davis

close to hers. In fact, they had been alone rarely, even when he'd been "courting" her, in his old fashioned way. He was still a very good-looking man. Pity he'd been through such bad luck on the marriage front.

"Are you living in the area again, Mrs. Webster?" He removed his fingers from her mouth so she could speak.

"No, I'm just here for a visit. I leave tomorrow."

"A pity, it would have been nice to have a chance to visit with an old friend. Do you and your husband have many children?"

"No. We never had children. And I'm not Mrs. Webster, actually, not anymore. Divorced." *Now why did she say that?*

"I am sorry to hear it. Divorce is a great sadness with which I am not unfamiliar."

"Scourge of the 20th century."

"A most terrible thing. Open please."

Dr. Falud picked away with his sharp little stick. It made a sickening, grinding noise. Alice gripped the armrests. She closed her eyes. Willing herself to relax. She felt his hand on her arm and her eyes flew open.

"You are not nervous, I hope?"

"Nervous?"

"You mentioned you are very afraid of dental work."

"Oh. No. I'm fine."

"You needn't be nervous. It is nothing at all, I am sure." He patted her shoulder. "I will just check to see if the filling can be moved at all. If not, all that is required is that the filling be filed down slightly. Will that be all right?"

"If you say so."

"Very good, just relax. Lie back and open wide for me, I won't hurt you."

And the check's in the mail, she thought.

In several pain-free minutes they were done.

"All finished. That was not so bad now, was it?"

"I was sure it was nothing, just one of those things I was afraid to let go by without doing something about it."

"I understand completely," said Dr. Falud. "I will let you

rinse your mouth and when you are finished I will be in the office."

She rinsed and walked across the hall.

"It really was very kind of you to see me special like this, Omar. Now, what do I owe you?"

"I would not think of charging you. Consider it a small service to an old acquaintance."

"That's so nice of you."

"Think nothing of it." He paused. "I hope I am not being too personal, but I would like to ask you..."

Here it comes. But did she want this? So soon after her train wreck of a divorce? Alice noticed a picture on the desk of a young girl, smiling, wind-tossed dark hair. Perfect teeth. She picked it up.

"Pretty girl," she said, stalling. "Is this your daughter? I remember her. She was what, eight, when we knew each other? She must be about thirty now? But she looks younger here, when was this taken?"

"Yes, Melanie is twenty-nine, but that is not Melanie, that is Noel..."

"Noel..." *probably not born then, Alice thought. Must be from marriage number two.* "I don't think we ever met."

"No, you would not have. She is my fiancée."

Where's the Demerol when you need it?

"Of course. How silly of me. She's lovely."

"Yes, she is very lovely."

"Congratulations. I'm sure you'll be very happy."

"Thank you. I am a very lucky man. Now, Mrs. Webster, as I was saying, a sad but true fact is that time takes a toll on us all. After a certain age the gums begin to recede and this can lead to all sorts of problems in later life. You really must discuss this with your regular dentist, your gums are much too sensitive..."

Cindy was waiting in the parking lot. She couldn't wait to hear all about her visit to the good doctor.

"So, how did it go?"

"It was just a teeny nick. Wear and tear, really."

"No, not that! The important stuff! Did he make a pass at you? He makes a pass at all the girls, he's quite famous for it."

"Oh course he did, dirty old man."

"And..."

"What do you think? I turned him down of course. I'm not that desperate!"

"Good for you. So what do you want to do tonight? Want to go to the club for dinner - see if Carlo's there? Or maybe we can hook you up with Fred's golf partner?"

"To be truthful, sweetie, I think I just want to take it easy tonight. I'm feeling sort of limp and a girl's got to get her beauty sleep."

"Not you, kiddo," said Cindy. "You still look like a teenager."

Calendar Waltz

1. January 17, 1996

Millicent Argyle stands at her husband Harold's coffin. She grips the mother of pearl clasp on her black purse so tightly she knows when she takes her hand away, a deep red furrow will be left, imprinted like a scar on her palm.

"Mama,... are you all right?" says her daughter Caroline, who comes up and puts a solicitous arm around her shoulder.

"I'll be fine dear, just leave me for a minute. Just leave me." She gently pushes the arm away.

Caroline looks back at her siblings, Cynthia and David, who'd urged her to do something about their mother. She'd been standing, glaring down at the body of their father, for far too long. People were noticing. She shrugs helplessly, and returns to her seat in the front row of the chapel.

Millicent is very angry, and this anger at her dead husband puzzles her. No one told her about this. She believed she should feel sorrow, and she did, in great stomach-lurching waves. But the anger's there too. Millicent's been angry ever since she

Lauren B. Davis

walked into the McClaren Funeral Home, three short days ago,
to pick out a casket for Harold's remains. The price of the acces-
sories of death is staggering. She's angry she should be in this
position at all - the pathetic and vaguely undignified position of
widow.

It is all Harold's fault. Because he died, she is now the
Widow Argyle, and she does not like it one bit. She doesn't like
being alone, which is uncharted territory, and she doesn't like
being filled with this festering rage, which she is. It's unbecoming
because, among other things, it binds her to him in a way she did
not wish to be bound.

Millicent Argyle takes a deep breath. She becomes aware
of the nervous shuffling, coughing, and general air of impatience
from the seats behind her. She turns to face them.

Keenly aware of the throbbing in the centre of her palm,
Millicent takes her seat, quietly, with no fuss whatsoever.

2. December 21, 1959

It's the year of the very cold winter. A real bone-cracker.
They have been married nearly eighteen years and Harold has
just announced, four days before Christmas, that he's leaving.
Absurdly, as Millicent looks out the kitchen window to confirm
that yes, Harold really has brought his secretary with him, she
thinks how cold the girl must be, out there in the Chevy. The
heater hasn't been working properly. The girl in the car turns on
the little overhead light near the rear-view mirror. Millicent can
see her powdering her nose. *What kind of a woman does that,
sitting in front of another woman's house, waiting for another
woman's husband?*

She can hear Harold in the bedroom, putting things in his
suitcase. He stumbles into something. Drops something. *Better
let the girl drive.*

Millicent suddenly feels sick to her stomach. Thank God
the kids are at that skating party. She closes her eyes and puts
both hands to her mouth. On the radio Nat King Cole sings

"...chestnuts roasting on an open fire...Jack frost nipping at your nose..." The smell of shortbread and almonds fills the kitchen, from the family room wafts the scent of the blue spruce Christmas tree. Millicent's holiday apron, the one with the holly and the angels embroidered on it, is suddenly too tight. She takes it off, wads it up into a ball and throws it. It unfurls in mid-air and flutters ineffectually to the black and white tiles on the floor.

Upstairs Harold curses as he barks his shin, probably on the cedar hope chest resting at the foot of their bed.

Millicent needs a drink. She kicks the apron as she walks past. Pours herself a stiff rye. Splashes a bit of Seven-Up into the glass. Gulps it. Feels it burn. She turns around when she hears Harold thumping down the stairs. She sees him. He holds the same suitcase they'd bought in Italy on their honeymoon.

"Millicent..." he starts, then falls silent.

"You bastard. You cold-hearted bastard."

"I'm going," he says.

"Then go, she's waiting out there, your little floozy."

"Tell the kids..."

"I'm not going to tell them anything. You tell them, you coward!"

"I'm going."

"Get out!"

Harold turns, walks to the door. He puts his hand on the knob and turns it. Millicent picks up the bottle of Seven-Up and throws it. It crashes into the wall not five inches from his head. He pulls into his collar like a turtle and runs out the door, slamming it behind him. The soda leaves a shiny trail down the wall to a festive pile of bright green glass. There is a good-sized dent in the wall.

3. April 3, 1960

Three months later, the dent is there for everyone to see... and so is Harold.

"Aren't you going to make Harold fix that dent?" asks Marge,

Lauren B. Davis

Millicent's best friend.

"He wanted to, but I stopped him," says Millicent, sipping her coffee and picking up the last of the brownie crumbs with her finger.

"God, why? I mean why be reminded of it all? He's been back for months."

"I know."

"So?"

"You know what I said to him? When he came upstairs with the paint and plaster? I said, 'I think we'll just leave it where it is, Harold. Should the occasion arise, I can use it as a gauge to see if my aim improves with practice.'"

"You didn't!"

"I did."

What she doesn't say is that she draws pleasure from knowing he had to see that skull-shaped dent in the wall every time he left the house. She doesn't need to keep bringing up the past. The writing is on the wall, so to speak.

4. September 24, 1990

With every passing year she thought one day, surely, they'd learn how to talk to each other. She kept trying.

"Harold, I know you don't want to talk about this," says Millicent, putting a plate holding a slice of cheesecake in front of him, "but I really need to discuss it."

"What is it?" He picks up the fork and tucks into his favourite dessert.

"I want to talk about money."

Silence.

"Harold, I want to talk about what would happen to me if you were to die first."

"You'll be fine."

"You keep saying that, but what do you mean?"

"I mean you'll have enough money."

"You know, I'd only get half your pension."

170

"The house is free and clear."

"Yes, but with everything going up the way it is, it would be very difficult with just half your pension."

"You'll be fine."

"You keep *saying* that!"

"Well," he says, putting down his fork, pushing his chair away from the table even though there is some cake left, "what more is there to discuss then? You won't have to worry about money."

Harold picks up the Sunday paper and walks downstairs.

5. February 23, 1996

Harold has been buried more than a month. Millicent lies in bed and worries about money.

I always worried about money. Someone had to.

Harold lied. There is no insurance. No stocks. No retirement savings bonds. There is social security, half his pension. She'll eat. She'll have clothes. She won't have to worry about a roof over her head, but she isn't going to spend her last years in any luxury, that's for sure.

Millicent rolls her face to the damp pillow. It's past noon. What's the point in getting up? She's a woman who built her life on doing for others, and now is no longer needed. There's no one left to take care of. And as annoying a man as Harold was, you could always rely on him to need something. How do you fill your days when no one's dependent on the results of your efforts?

Beds can remain unmade.

Dinner uncooked.

Mail can pile up.

Clothes can stay dirty.

One day slides into the next with nothing to differentiate it from the one before. Greyness and half-light. Sleep and half-life. No one had ever said how tired grief made you. How even swinging your legs over the side the bed takes Herculean effort.

Millicent is coming undone.

171

6. January 24, 1944

Harold Argyle stands in front of his mother's tiny white clapboard house, eyes squinting into the late afternoon sun. He holds himself up very tall and straight. His hat at just the right angle. On his right side is his cousin Gregory and on his left is his cousin Brian. They are both privates in the Royal Canadian Air Force. He is a captain. He's wearing his double-breasted greatcoat. All three have their arms rigidly at their sides and proud, beaming smiles on their faces. Harold's tie is crooked.

Millicent snaps the photo and starts to cry. Harold puts his arms around her and the cousins leave them alone for the few minutes before they have to leave for the station.

"Don't cry, Pet, it's all right," he says. She barely comes up to his shoulder and her face is buried in his coat. He cradles her head.

"I love you, I love you, I love you," she says.

"I love you, too. So much."

"I wouldn't be able to keep going..."

"No, no, Millie, none of that now. It won't last long now and I'll be back before you know it."

"Promise me."

"I promise."

They stand like that, close as cloth and skin will allow, until Brian clears his throat and says it's time to go.

Millicent has the photo developed and sleeps with it under her pillow until Harold comes home, then she has it framed in silver and puts it on the mantel in the living room.

7. April 18, 1996

Their father has been dead three months. In Caroline's kitchen, Millicent's children meet, to discuss what's to be done about Mother.

"Mummy needs to take responsibility for herself," says Cynthia, the youngest.

"Dad's only been dead a couple of months, Cyn!" says David, the middle.

"But if Mom had taken some responsibility earlier, she wouldn't be feeling like this now. I mean, you can't just hand over all your power to someone and then whine when you don't like the way they handle things."

"God, but you can be judgmental!" says Caroline, the oldest. She refills glasses from a second bottle of Merlot. "Women didn't do that in their generation. The men took care of these things. That's the way it was."

"Well, she needs to take care of her own finances now. I can't believe she never even had her own bank account."

"Fine for you," says Caroline. "Might I suggest you take some of your own advice? I mean just how much money did you borrow from them last year?"

"Hey!"

"Come on, you guys," says David. "What I'm worried about is not her finances, her finances are fine, although she may not believe so. What I'm worried about is this apathy she's slipped into. She's giving up."

"She's *crippled* up. Angry. She's bitter," says Caroline.

"About what, for Christ's sake?" says David.

"What do you think, jeez, Dave, where you been?" says Cynthia.

Caroline looks at David archly, over the top of her horn-rim glasses. "Try an unfaithful husband who drank them out of a cushy retirement."

"Oh for God's sake, not that again. Dad was sober for what, twenty years, when he died? And as for the rest, I'm not sure I even believe everything she says, but even so, it was a long time ago. You're not telling me she's still blaming him for all the unhappiness in her life?"

"You see," says Cynthia, "that's what I mean, she needs to take responsibility."

After three more hours of going around in the same circles, the only thing they decide is that David will make up a budget for Millicent and Caroline will have her to dinner more often. Cynthia's leaving for California in two weeks, so she won't be able to help too much, but she does commit to calling her mother, as often as her schedule permits.

8. June 12, 1996

Ingrid Fletcher calls Millicent to see how she's doing. To ask if she's read the book on grieving she dropped off a few weeks ago.

"No, I tried, Ingrid, and it is very kind of you, but I just can't seem to keep my mind on anything."

"Well, I'm sure you'll start feeling better soon. It is such a shock. Are you getting out at all?"

"A bit. I don't see the kids as much as I'd like."

"Ah, that's too bad, but it's typical isn't it?"

"I suppose." Another of those awkward silences so many of her conversations are filled with. "How's Phil?"

"Oh, he's fine, golfing all the time."

"You going up to the cottage this summer?"

"For a week or so in July, and weekends. If it weren't for that lake we'd probably never see the grandkids."

"That'll be nice."

"Well, dear, I just wanted to see how you were. We're thinking of you, but I must run. You take good care of yourself."

"I will. Thanks for calling."

Millicent knew it would be like this. She's the first among her friends to win the title Widow. She's no longer suitable company, despite all their death-bed pledges to the contrary. Harold was allowed to die without any concern as to her well-being, as though she were a child to be parcelled off to friends for care and feeding. After the funeral they disappeared back into their secure lives, matched as bookends, holding each other up with assurances they had many good years together yet. She became a sad reminder of their coming separations, of their messy mortalities.

She's a third wheel, an extra unattached female. As though she'd want any of their dried up old men! She'd had enough of all that nonsense. It was never worth as much as all the fuss made over it any way.

Millicent walks from the living room into the bedroom, but then can't remember why. She bursts into tears.

9. July 17, 1996

Millicent sits in front of the kitchen window watching the neighbour's beagle yank at the end of its tether every time a kid rides by. She's drinking yesterday's heated-up coffee and half listening to a radio talk show about rape.

"There's no way," a woman's voice says, "no way in the world I'm going to let that scum bag have the last word. I will not let him ruin my life. I will not spend the rest of my time on this planet cringing behind a locked door."

"That's a good attitude," said the show's commentator, a relentlessly chirpy female psychiatrist. "Don't let resentment and fear imprison you. You need to work through the emotions and begin to take steps out into the world again. Claim your birthright as a fully alive human being."

"But it's hard sometimes. There are days I want to just crawl into the back of my closet with a bottle of Jack Daniels and stay there."

"Fight it, girl! Be a warrior in your own life! Be courageous! You're not alone. Millions of women have experienced what you have and they have overcome it. So can you."

Millicent switches off the radio. She has always had contempt for people classified as victims. Survivors, that was a better word. Survivors earn respect. Victims earn nothing but pity, and that simply won't do.

Millicent curls her hair and puts on a nice skirt and blouse. She drives herself to the shopping mall, determined to have lunch and a walk through the stores. When she arrives, all she sees are couples. She makes it back to the car before she collapses in tears, but she can't face it. She goes home again.

Lauren B. Davis

10. September 30, 1996

After the episode at the shopping mall, she had some bad weeks, but she manages to keep the house clean. She shops. She eats. She listens to David prattle on about money and understands none of it. She listens to Caroline's advice about getting a part-time job, doing volunteer work, getting a dog.

To Caroline she says, "None of this is fair. It isn't fair that Harold died at seventy-five when his mother lived to be eighty-seven, his sister's eighty-four and still globe-trotting without a care apparently. It isn't fair your father didn't take better care of the finances when he promised me he would. It isn't fair I've got aches and pains in all sorts of places I never even knew I had before. Normal bodily functions are an adventure in discomfort. And I'm so lonely I could scream. And you know what? Sometimes I do! The golden years? Phooey. You can have 'em."

She sees the look of embarrassment and worry on her daughter's face.

"Oh, pay me no attention. I'm just not used to being alone so much. I'm fine. Don't worry, dear."

Her daughter gives her a relieved smile and promises to have her over to dinner next week.

11. December 24, 1996

Millicent has refused to see her children for Christmas. They may be angry and hurt, but it's what she wants. She doesn't want to spend the day wrapped up in tears, but she probably will, and she'd rather do that alone. She's tired of people looking at her like they're afraid she's going to suddenly lose her mind right there in front of them. She wants to be by herself.

She plans to cook herself some coq-au-vin and open a bottle of wine. She's rented four movies to watch on the VCR David bought her. She doesn't want to watch all those sappy Christmas movies. If she sees *It's a Wonderful Life* one more time, she'll throw something through the television.

She's so tired of being angry. She's so tired of being so sad.

That night she wraps up the charm bracelet Harold gave her for their fifth wedding anniversary. It's gold and filled with charms. She never wears it anymore because it's so heavy and with her arthritis it hurts her wrist. Harold filled the bracelet up with charms from all the places he travelled on business, to prove she was always on his mind. There were charms from when each of their children was born and charms of little gardening tools, for she loved to garden, and a little book charm, and a tiny caged bird, and a painter's palette, and a little golden angel...

She wraps it in beautiful paper like an illuminated page from the Book of Kells and ties it with a midnight blue silk ribbon. She sets it on her bedside table, next to the photo of Harold and his two cousins, dressed to go away to war.

It's the only present she'll unwrap tomorrow.

12. February 15, 1997

9:34 a.m. Millicent finds herself sitting, staring at the kitchen table, which is covered in crumbs of food she doesn't remember eating. In front of her is another endlessly grim grey day. The walls of the room seem to tilt inwards over her head. She isn't sure what day it is. She looks at the morning paper sitting unread on the counter. Thursday. What happened to Wednesday?

I've got to stop this. I'm disappearing. Millicent hauls herself up and stands in the middle of the floor, taking deep, deep breaths, just to feel the sensation of air in her lungs, of her heart beating. What has she been waiting for? A bell to go off, or the pain to stop, or someone to come and rescue her, someone to notice how dreadful her life is and say they were sorry for all her trouble? *Ridiculous old woman. Haven't you had enough?*

1:25 p.m. Millicent Argyle steps into the gymnasium at the Pembroke Senior Citizen Centre, where the line-dancing class is scheduled to begin in five minutes. She's wearing the bright fuchsia pantsuit of a woman who will not be intimidated. She isn't going to end up a monstrous old woman sitting in front of the television, hoping an aluminium siding salesman would call just so she'd have someone to talk to.

There are perhaps thirty-five people in the room, almost all women who seem to know each other. Millicent thinks it's typical no one comes over to introduce themselves as she stands alone in a corner, clutching her good beige leather purse. She should put the purse down, but where? Someone is sure to steal it if she leaves it on a chair.

She thinks coming here may have been a mistake. As though she'll even be able to remember how to dance! It's been years since she has danced and she has no expectation that the tap classes of her youth will suddenly pay off by leaping to memory and taking control of her feet. Her face begin to flush red and fusses in her purse for a Kleenex with which to blow her nose.

1:35 p.m. Sally Richardson, the teacher, comes in singing out a cheery hello and scattering across the floor with the whirl-wind effect of someone who's always late for everything. She carries one of the big boom boxes the kids all have growing out of their heads these days. She looks about fifty and impossibly trim and stringy in the way of over-exercised, underfed women of a certain age. People start taking their places around the gym floor.

Millicent stands where she is, still holding her purse. She realises most of the women are wearing pouches around their hips. One woman, whose hair is the sort of red that never appears in nature, wears a small white patent leather back pack, which would look very fashionable on a sixteen year-old. Millicent can't go through the class clutching her purse, yet she doesn't want to leave it at the back of the room where anyone can make off with it.

Millicent takes a deep breath. She squares her shoulders. She marches to the front of the room, and places her purse next to the big tape recorder the teacher's setting up in front of the mirrors lining one wall. She'll be able to keep her eye on it there. No one would dare steal it from the front of the class.

She turns around and comes face to face with a wall of people standing ready for the music to begin. All eyes are on her, the newcomer. Her legs turn to cream of wheat and she feels trapped, pinned to the mirror by all those eyes. For a moment she's afraid she'll start to cry.

"Excuse me, you're new to the class aren't you? Why don't you take a place in the front so you can see the steps clearly?" says Sally, a big yellow-toothed smile on her make-up spackled face.

"Oh, no! No thank you... No. I'll just go to the back where I can watch the others and get my bearings."

"OK, as you wish. Nice to have you with us."

"Yes, right. Thank you." Her face is flaming. Why on earth is she thanking this poultry-necked woman? She walks, feeling like a retirement home Moses, as the multicoloured sea of jogging suits and fringe and gold decorated oversized T-shirts parts to make room for her.

"Here, why don't you stay next to Connie and me? But we're both hopeless at this, so I can't promise you'll learn anything from watching us. I'm Pamela Hutchison." A woman with white hair swept back from her face and the bluest eyes Millicent has ever seen holds out her hand.

"Millicent Argyle. Thank you." What a lovely smile this woman has. Millicent wonders if those are her real teeth. "I haven't danced in years. I'm sure I'll never catch on."

"It takes a wee bit, but you'll get it. Don't panic."

Good advice, Millicent decides. She takes a deep breath, and exhales slowly.

The music begins - something by Barry Manilow. It's catchy. A good beat. Sally claps her hands and taps her foot. One, two, three, four...

"OK, folks, here we go! Now watch me first. Right step, cross, step, ball and chain, step, stop, clap! Again, Right step, cross, step, ball and chain, step, stop, clap. OK, got it?"

All around the room, people take tiny steps and work out in their heads the series of moves. Millicent takes a few tentative steps. She thinks she has it.

"Let's give it a try, now, one, two, three, four...RIGHT step, cross..."

"Take a peep at Frank and Sylvia, over there in the matching blue and white," Pamela says. "He absolutely hates coming and gets dragged every week by Sylvia. He looks like an old rooster, scratching away at the homestead floor." She giggles.

Millicent looks over and sees a tall, hunched-over, skinny man, in baggy synthetic blue jogging pants and matching jacket. He has a long nose and receding chin and puffs of grey hair fizzling up over each ear. With his arms held awkwardly cocked up at the elbows, Millicent is forced to agree, he does indeed look like an irritable barnyard fowl. She finds herself grinning.

The music starts again and Millicent takes one step and then another. She feels her muscles stretch out, compliant and pleasingly obedient. It feels good. She feels light on her feet. She begins to feel the first twinges of pride in herself, in her bravery. She puts a little extra sway in her hips, a little *ooomph* in her shoulders. Next to her, Pamela takes a misstep and collides into Connie and they both collapse into fits of laughter.

1:47 p.m. Millicent Argyle dances.

Party Girls

My mother's eyes were flat, cold, fish-eyes. No doubt about it, she was going to hit me.

She'd kept her mouth clamped shut all morning and all through lunch. She refused to speak to me but she still made a lot of noise. She kept slamming cupboard doors and slapping cutlery onto the table. Finally she couldn't keep quiet anymore and I was just as glad to have her break the silence. Get it over with.

"I saw you last night," she said. "Kissing him on the street where all the neighbours could see you." She snorted. "You have no shame."

"I didn't do anything wrong," I said.

"You're nothing but a slut," she said. Her head jutted and all the cords in her throat stood out.

I pointed my finger at her and said "Don't you EVER call me that again!"

It was the finger that did it.

I might have got away with the words, but not that finger. It poked out into the no man's land between us and crossed over the boundary. It was an act of war.

I could have told her that at Peter's party last night Debbie tried to get me to lie on the bed with her and Peter and a guy named Mike who was reputed to have the biggest dick in Southfield High. I could have told her how I did let Mike kiss me for a minute but then I got really scared and wanted to get out of the room. I could have told her how Mike didn't want to let me go and how if it hadn't been for Peter I don't know what would have happened. I could have told her how I was shaking and how Peter put his arm around me and said how sorry he was. And he was, I could tell because he was shaking too. He took me out of the room and we left Debbie and Mike on the bed, her fat ass up in the air in skin-tight jeans as she rocked back and forth on top of him. I said I wanted to go home and he said he'd walk me. On the way we didn't say much. I think he was embarrassed. When we got in front of my house I said, "Thanks."

"Look, I'm really sorry," he said. "Things get out of hand with Debbie sometimes. When she brought you to the party, I just figured,… you know." He stuck his hands in his pockets and squinched up his eyes.

My face was so hot I thought my hair was on fire. "Yeah, I know. But I'm not into that stuff, OK?" I said.

"Better than OK," he said.

I liked his smile.

"I better go in," I said.

"Maybe I'll see you tomorrow," he said.

"Yeah, maybe," I said. "Thanks again." Then I put my hands on his shoulders and reached way up and gave him a kiss. Just a small one. Just so he knew I wasn't a complete baby.

I could have told her that, but I didn't.

My Mum was tiny, no more than five feet and no more than a hundred pounds with her pockets full of nails, but she could really pack a wallop when she wanted to. As soon as I looked over my pointed finger into her face, I could see it coming. She drew back and slapped me. But it wasn't too hard and it was more on my shoulder than my face. Maybe it was because she didn't come at me full force that made me think I should fight back this time. I don't know. Anyway, I slapped her back. On the arm, but I slapped her.

For a minute she just stood there staring at me with her mouth open. Then her hands flew everywhere and I guess mine did too. She was yelling and crying and I was crying and trying to keep her off me and nobody was really getting hurt but it sure felt like we were.

I couldn't believe I'd raised my hand to her. I wasn't even allowed to raise my *voice*. If my face showed I was mad she called me Chief Thundercloud and laughed at me. Which made me even madder. So mad sometimes I thought my insides would explode and I had to dig my nails into my palms and count backward from a hundred until I could get somewhere alone.

Dad always said Mum's nerves were bad and the best thing to do was just give her a wide berth when she got "that way". Easy for him to say, with an office to go to and a job full of travel and a world full of bars and clients to be wooed.

"No kid of mine," she kept repeating with each slap. "No kid of mine."

We heard his footsteps on the stairs. We turned around at the same time and saw Dad standing in the door, his hair greasy and cowlicked from his long time in bed, little white spots of dried saliva in both corners of his lips. He still looked puffy from last night. The broken blood vessels along his nose stood out bright and angry.

He pulled down the corners of his mouth. For a second he looked like he was about to say something but he didn't. He turned around, the *Sunday Star* folded up under his arm, and he went downstairs to the rec room where the TV and the liquor cabinet were.

We stood staring after him and then my mother started to make a moaning noise deep down in her throat and I thought she was going to start screaming at him, but she didn't. I waited to see what she'd do next. I sort of wanted to reach out to touch her, but she turned away from me and blew her nose into an already damp Kleenex.

"Get out of here. I don't want to see you," she said.

So I left, the corners of my mouth twitching with guilt, pulling down into the strain of tears coming. I wished I had a sister or big brother or even a dog. I ducked through the side gate and down the alley. I didn't want to bump into Mrs. Greeson and have to answer her stupid questions about how my Mum was getting along these days.

"Your Ma feeling better these days, Missy?" she'd call out from her post on the front porch, her blue hair stiff and shiny like it might have been sprayed with Windex and her voice all sticky-sweet.

"She's fine, Mrs. Greeson."

"You ever need anything, dear, you know I'm here."

I couldn't handle it today.

Usually I went over to Debbie's when our house blew up. But I wasn't in the mood to hear all the details of the gooey fun I'd walked out on last night. So I went over to the park across from Peter's house and eventually he came out and we hung around and talked for a while and he asked me if I wanted to come over to his place for a barbecue next Saturday when his aunt and uncle and cousins were coming over and I said OK. I felt shy around him, but I liked the idea of having plans. Of having something to do next weekend. Something that was mine.

I got back before six and the house was quiet. My Dad was still downstairs with the TV on and my mother was in her room. I stuck a frozen vegetarian pizza in the oven, ate it and washed up my plate. Then went up to bed even though it was really early. I took a deep breath before I stopped at my mother's room.

"Hi," I said.

"Hello," she said, lockjawed. She didn't look up from *Good Housekeeping*.

"I'm sorry," I said, because somebody had to and that's my job.

"Me too," she said. "Did you eat something?"

"Yeah."

"Your father still downstairs?"

"Yeah, I think so," I said.

"Figures," she said. "Bastard."

And we didn't say anything else.

The Golden Benefactors Of Brewster McMahon

Brewster McMahon was born deaf and he never made a sound at all, neither a whimper nor a whine, neither a grunt nor a giggle. He never hiccupped, coughed or sneezed. His joints did not pop and his stomach did not growl. The only way to know he was in the land of the living at all was to put your ear against his chest and hear the beating of his heart. A thing his mother did many times when he was just a wee tyke, lying silent and joyful in the cradle.

He walked with a silent step, scaring the bejeebers out of more than one St. Melwyn's housewife. Mrs. Reilly, for example, now and then when she hung out her wash, felt she was being watched, only to spin around, a clothespin in her hand like a child's make-believe dagger, and find Brewster standing there, a load of smoked haddies to sell in a wicker basket under his arm and a sheepish grin on his face, for he never meant to scare a soul.

"Brewster McMahon!" she'd exclaim, with a hand to her floury bosom, "you'll be the death of me, boy! Can you not learn to whistle or something?"

She pursed her lips to show him how, but she looked so funny, he threw back his head and laughed in his soundless way and nearly dropped the fish.

This silent way of being was indeed a remarkable thing, but it was not the only remarkable thing. The other was that your man Brewster could see the spirits of the dead. He didn't, how-ever, like to think of them as the dead, considering that to be an altogether unfriendly term. It sounded far too lugubrious for these ephemeral, delicate creatures, and one which did nothing to describe the great care and love they had for the living. He pre-ferred to think of them as the Golden Benefactors.

Early on, Brewster learned that only he saw these luminous creatures. As a child he would point and laugh and reach out to the shining figures all around the room, delighted to be the centre of so much attention.

"What in the name of heaven's that boy staring at?" his father would say, tapping his pipe on the rim of the ashtray.

"I wish I knew," said his mother. "You'd best ask the cat. The Blessed Mother herself only knows, but whatever it is, I think Minkins can see it too." Mrs. McMahon made the sign of the cross and sipped her tea.

Minkins, the calico cat, sat next to the boy, stared at thin air, raised her velvet paw, claws tucked away, and batted as though a piece of string were dangled there. Brewster clapped his hands and opened his mouth in a wide, toothless, silent smile.

When he was seven his father took him to see the priest, just to be sure. Father O'Brien said there was not a thing wrong with the boy.

"If it's anything at all, and I'm not saying it is, mind, but if it were, it would be the angels of heaven watching out for him, making up for the terrible sorrow of his poor wee ears."

"So, it's not the Devil that's after him Father, you're sure."

"Don't be daft man, the child's a cherub! One of God's own lambs, can you not see it?"

Mr. McMahon looked at the tousle-haired, sturdy-legged little boy, his eyes the colour of a sweet May sky, and a smile that could charm the birds in the trees, and was sure he was blessed, even though it was hard to accept he'd die without ever hearing the boy call him 'Da'.

He drew a rough hand over his heavy chin and clumsy features. "He's like a new soul to the world, all innocent and him never learned to even cry. He's such a lovely boy, it's true, but odd, with all his staring, as at ghosts, like."

"Sure, he's half in Heaven," said the priest.

As Brewster grew he came to love the world of the sea and the deep woods. He knew every foxhole, owl's nest and badger's sett and the villagers thought he had the fairy way with animals and fish. Perhaps, they mused, in his soundless world he had learned to understand the secret language of God's creatures. They said the fish fair jumped into his boat of their own accord.

Brewster grew to be tall and strong. He smiled easily and was never known to harm a soul, although now and then there were those who were uneasy around him, as though he knew something about them of which they themselves ought to be a little ashamed.

Danny the Pot, for example, so-called for his insatiable hunger for poker. Danny's great-uncle Micah hovered around him like a grand gold moth, all the time trying to keep Danny from setting foot back inside Jackman's pub, where a back-room poker game drew Danny like a sulphur flame. Uncle Micah hid Danny's boots, and made the baby laugh and reach out to her father, and he helped Danny's wife find a new hiding spot for his weekly wages, but it was no good at all. Danny was determined and nothing his dead great-uncle could do kept him from it.

Brewster wished he could dry the spirit's tears as he saw him following after Danny in the early morning hours, Danny's pockets empty again and his temper a fist-forming cloud of fury around his head. Danny saw him as he passed and shook his club-like hand at him.

"Go on with you, you dumb-mouthed ghoul," he said, "or I'll make you see stars!"

Brewster couldn't understand the words, but he took their meaning well enough and shook his head as long-dead Micah cried harder than ever.

More often than not the Benefactors would win the day. Like the time Annie Beechum nearly walked out in front of the horses and only stopped for moment to tie her shoe which had somehow become untied, and therefore missed having her skull cracked open on the paving stones and a hoof-mark on her breast.

Or the time old Calum Tremain, who never said a kind word to man nor beast, lay on his deathbed. His own dead mother, a sparkling form by the bedstead, reached over and touched her honey-flamed fingertip to her aged son's mouth. He began, at last, and not a moment too soon, to say how sorry he was for the pain he'd caused and how much, even though he'd been an ornery old bugger and hadn't shown it, he'd loved his gentle wife Katie and their two red-haired daughters.

Brewster grew up being an observer of those whose caring influenced the lives of men and women, and he wondered at it. It was a marvel he could never explain and he knew he was blessed to witness it. It was a good life, if sometimes a lonely one. It was easy to forget him, silent as he was, and sometimes he felt more like a ghost himself.

When he was thirty-five or so, on a night much colder than it should be for that early in November, Brewster sat on the porch of his cottage, shielded from the wind and wearing the heavy sweater his mother had made for him. He looked up from the net he was repairing so as to see the last of the shafts of purple and rose and daffodil light dipping below the horizon. From the corner of his eye he caught a movement and looked toward the village. He saw a crowd of people standing in a frantic group by the butcher's. He rose and took his coat from the hook by the door. He walked toward them, curious to see what all the hubbub was about.

A woman he didn't know stood in the middle of the group, wringing her hands, her hair flying about her, wild and mad. Next to her stood Mrs. Flannery, and as they looked so much alike, Brewster thought they must be related. Mrs. Flannery tried to calm her down.

"It's my boy, my Liam, my Liam," she wailed, turning round and round in circles like a trapped thing, "he's lost, he's lost and night coming on!"

"Calm down now, Mrs. We'll find your boy," said a man.

She wailed again, her hands now pulling at her clothes in a frenzy of grief. "If I loose the boy too, I'll go mad, I swear I will, I shall go mad!"

"Hush, now, hush Sara, they'll find him," said Mrs. Flannery and tried to stop her tearing at herself.

"But the cold, the cold, and him so small!"

"Tell us where you saw him last," said Mr. Mack, the butcher.

"At the end of the meadow behind the cottage, where the rabbits have a warren..." She paused, her eyes wide, "Oh, sweet Mary, the woods, he'll have wondered into the woods!" And with that she began to scream and no one could console her.

Danny the Pot puffed himself up like a man in charge and said, "Right men, we'll form groups of five and branch out. Ring the church bells, round up everyone you can."

"Jesus," muttered Mr. Mack to Father O'Brien, "with this early storm coming in, Father, I hope you're praying."

But as Father O'Brien had already started, he didn't stop to answer.

Brewster understood none of this, of course, but he could tell something was dreadfully wrong, and guessed that someone was in terrible danger. Everyone was in a panic. Everyone, including the Golden Ones.

Someone bumped into Brewster. It was Danny the Pot.

"Get out of the way if you can't be of any help, you great idiot!" he said.

Brewster was as familiar with all the spirits present as he was with the living, except for one, and that was a damp-looking figure standing near the distraught woman. When the new, unknown spirit saw Brewster looking at him he left the woman and moved toward Brewster until he stood in front of him and looked directly into his eyes. Brewster looked back, trying to understand.

Then a marvellous thing began.

Inside Brewster's head, right next to his thoughts, was something new. It was impossible to describe, but Brewster knew he had been waiting for it all his life. It was as though the spirit had reached inside Brewster's skull and begun to spin and draw golden circles and swirls. His body vibrated and his soul rejoiced. It was in his head, this new thing, but it was in his heart too, and his arms and legs and veins and skin and hair. It was the secret of everything, whatever it was.

Brewster smiled. The spirit looked relieved. He began to point urgently at the shore and the cliffs that rose there, to the west, where the caves were. The spirit pointed to the woman, pointed to the cliffs. He reached out to Brewster in supplication and Brewster understood.

Brewster ran from man to man, pulling on shirtsleeves and pointing to the cliffs. They brushed him aside in their hurry to find the missing child. He grabbed lapels and pointed to the cliffs. They pushed past him. He reached out and took hold of Danny the Pot as he stood in the middle of the street, directing traffic. He shook him and pointed at the cliffs. Danny knocked him down and kicked him.

"I'll not tell you again Brewster McMahon," he yelled, "get home with you! Out of our way, or I'll knock you down again!"

Brewster picked himself up and stood helplessly, his arms out in front of him, begging. But it was no good. They couldn't hear him.

Brewster looked for the spirit. He was far down the shore, gesturing Brewster to follow him. Brewster ran. He knew the sea; there was little time. The tide was turning fast and soon the path to the cliffs would be cut off. If someone were up there, they would be trapped.

When he reached the base of the cliffs, the spirit began to climb. The waves came in a little more and a little more with every pulse. The sand path was already gone; Brewster had to scramble on the rocks. He looked up to the horizon. It was black and churning with wind and cloud. His heart pounded very hard, but he kept concentrating on the new thing in his head and the stones beneath his hands and feet.

Brewster climbed up to the rocky crag just in time, for the waves came crashing in behind him and closed off any hope of escape. He knew there was no turning back now, not until the tide turned. Hand over hand he climbed, following the figure in front of him, careful not to slip on the sloping, slippery stones. The way was treacherous, with the wind whipped up and the spray and his quickly numbing fingers. The figure skipped easily, his feet hardly touching the rocks at all, urging Brewster to hurry on.

At last Brewster came to the entrance of the furthest of the cliff caves and, when his eyes had adjusted to the dark, saw inside a small boy, shivering and rolled up into a tiny ball. Brewster moved to him quickly and picked him up, light as a feather. The child looked up into Brewster's face.

"I only came to see if I could find my Da," said the boy, and he cried icy tears. "I'm a good climber."

Brewster held the child close, wrapping his great arms around him. He rocked him back and forth and back and forth and slowly felt the child's body begin to warm, drinking in all the red glow from Brewster's enormous heart. The stones beneath him were very cold. The wind shook the sea and sent icy blasts deep into the cave. It was very dark. The storm was much worse now and the temperature dropping.

Liam concentrated on the beating of Brewster's heart and Brewster concentrated on the glorious new thing in his head.

The villagers looked all over the woods, carrying torches and calling as they went. They looked in every tree and hollow and hummock they could think of, but they had no luck. By the time anyone thought to look in the cliff caves, it was too late to go by land, and too stormy to go by sea. They had to wait for morning.

At first light they reached the caves and found the boy and the man, tightly wrapped together in the great man's coat, his arms locked around the boy. It took two men to pry the arms away, for the rigor mortis had set in.

"Is the boy all right?" called out one man.

"I think he is, by God, I think he is," called another.

"Let the mother through, let her through," cried a third.

Lauren B. Davis

Mrs. Flannery's cousin's ran to her son and scooped him up, taking no notice, in her frenzy, of the shape of Liam's saviour, motionless as the rocks themselves. Cooing at the child and patting him all over to make sure he really was alive and safe, she let herself be helped down the path to a waiting cart, frantic to get the boy in front of a fire.

The men stood around the still form of Brewster, whose back was to the cave mouth, so he would have taken the brunt of the storm's freezing blast.

"God, if only we'd listened to him," said a man.

"Oh, if only we'd understood," said another.

"Imagine him staying with the child like that," said Danny the Pot.

Father O'Brien closed his eyes and said the sacrament.

The men looked at each other, fidgeted, and none of them asked what they all wondered. *How did he know?*

At Mrs. Flannery's cottage Liam was wrapped in shawls and comforters and propped in front of the hearth with a cup of camomile tea. Mrs. Flannery and her cousin sat at the table, holding hands, and prayed for the soul of the man who gave his body's warmth to save the boy.

"And I didn't even stop to pay my respect, so worried was I about Liam," said the cousin.

"Oh, but I'm sure everyone understands," said Mrs. Flannery. "You were half out of your mind with worry. It's normal."

"I'll have a stone carved for him, sure it's the least I can do."

"That'd be grand."

They sat quietly for a moment until they realised the child was humming a tune. Mrs. Flannery's cousin's eyes flew open and her hand flew to her mouth. The song continued sweet and sad. She stood, upsetting the stool on which she sat.

"What is it, Sara?" said Mrs. Flannery, going to her cousin.

"Why, that's the very lullaby his own father made up for him. He used to sing it every night when Liam was just a babe. But he was too young to remember. He wasn't even two years when his Da was lost at sea!" She ran to the boy.

"Liam, are you all right, my pet?"

"Yes Mummy, I'm all warm now."

"That song, Precious... that song... wherever did you hear it?"

Liam looked up at her and smiled. "Brewster taught me," he said.

"Brewster?" The mother looked uncomprehendingly at her cousin.

"It's not possible," said Mrs. Flannery.

"That was his name," said Liam. "He told me, and he said music was his favourite thing in all the world."

"Sweet Jesus, Mary and Joseph," cried Mrs. Flannery, and would have fallen on the floor for certain, had not a chair miraculously appeared behind her.

About the Author

Lauren Davis was born in Montreal and now lives in Paris with her husband, Ron. She studied writing at the University of Indiana and at the Humber School of Creative Writing. A contributing editor at *WRITE MAGAZINE,* her work has appeared in *EXILE, OFFSHOOTS, POTPOURRI, THE QUEEN STREET QUARTERLY, ROOM OF ONE'S OWN,* and*THE LAZY WRITER.*